The

RHEEA MUKHERJEE

Body

A NOVEL

Myth

The Unnamed Press
Los Angeles, CA

AN UNNAMED PRESS BOOK

www.unnamedpress.com

Unnamed Press, and the colophon, are registered trademarks of Unnamed Media LLC.

Library of Congress Cataloging-in-Publication Data
Names: Mukherjee, Rheea, author.
Title: The body myth : a novel / Rheea Mukherjee.
Description: First edition. l Los Angeles : Unnamed Press, 2019.
Identifiers: LCCN 2018060364 l ISBN 9781944700843 (pbk.)
Classification: LCC PS3613.U388 B63 2019 l DDC 813/.6--dc23
LC record available at https://lccn.loc.gov/2018060364

ISBN: 978-1-944700-84-3
eISBN: 978-1-944700-93-5

Designed and typeset by Jaya Nicely
Cover artwork by Rachel Levit Ruiz

The excerpt from a letter by Michel Foucault, from the book *Friendship as a Way of Life: Foucault, AIDS, and the Politics of Shared Estrangement* by Tom Roach, is reprinted by permission from the State University of New York Press © 2012, State University of New York. All rights reserved.

The poems "It Felt Love" and "Faithful Lover", from the Penguin Publication *The Gift: Poems by Hafiz* by Daniel Ladinsky, © 1999, are used with permission of the author.

Distributed by Publishers Group West
Manufactured in the United States of America

First Edition

Some might say there isn't anything beyond this physical world

Too late for you to see

This one's for you, Dad

I know you still see

The Body Myth

I

Take my story like you would a large pill. Place it on your tongue and swallow it in one gulp. I intend to write the truth. Truth is perspective, and I have been scrupulous with mine. The ego may occasionally sway me, persuade me to write lines that amplify my individual contribution. It might shelter you from certain details and obscure the things I am not proud of. But like most things, in good time, the truth always emerges.

When I look back, I see myself as an Indian city on the verge of finding an identity. And then I lost control, expanded without direction, without a plan, becoming a vast series of interconnected roads, chaotic lanes, and fumes that left my body and mind exhausted. It's true, every love story has been told. Every hidden kiss, every love letter, every heartbreak, accounted for and documented—it's been said. Mine is no exception, but like everything else my version will exist as well. To get it right, I'll start at the beginning. Love stories, they deserve to be told—the way they bloomed, every little etch on the soul, every shift in the core, every fuck—like it was last night.

Suryam, like most Indian cities, was hot in the summer and cooler in the winter, the rains unpredictable. We did have one thing that no other town, city, or village had: the Rasagura fruit. Pink on the outside, yellow on the inside, and speckled with tiny brown seeds, Rasagura thrived in Suryam's microclimate and no other. It was written about far too much, as its exoticization demanded. Its replication has been tried, of course, in the fertile soils of many other places, here in India and around the world, to unfortunate results. No, there was something in the soul of the city that made its way into the soil and extended to the rural outskirts, the end of the Rasagura's dominion. There was even a border sign: LEAVING THE LAND OF RASAGURA. There was enough to share. Heaps of Rasagura were brought to market each day by the truckload, and other cities and towns bought the fruit at prices that would cover a fancy dinner.

What does it taste like? Like a soaked berry, bursting with the tang of a lemon, with the texture of pudding and the sweetness of mango. The chief minister had tried to rename the city Rasagura in its honor, but it never came together. Still, the people of Suryam took credit, smiled proudly at relatives as they brought them baskets of the fruit. Dutifully, people from others cities said the same old thing, again and again, *Ah, how lucky you are to live where the Rasagura grows.*

We didn't feel lucky; it was, after all, an ordinary Indian city with weak infrastructure and a bunch of people in a hurry. We didn't think about the Rasagura all that much, only when other people brought it up, or when we read another article with a new scientific theory for its hyper-local growth. Rasagura. The name could be seen in other places too: pharmacies, gas stations, general stores—all named after a fruit. It was no different from any of our overused Hindu god names: Ganesha, Shiva, Lakshmi. And yet, once in a while, Rasagura succeeded in making us feel superior. The type of vicarious pride you feel when someone from your country wins, say, a Nobel Prize.

Otherwise, the fruit is just there, and I'll try not to mention it too much. I digress just to find the right moment to start my story, and talking about the Rasagura, for some reason, helps. But the Rasagura certainly has nothing to do with it. No, my story starts with Sara.

The First Time I Saw Sara

The woman was sitting on a park bench in West Point Gardens, where I came every Sunday for a five-kilometer walk. She couldn't see me, but I had stopped midstride to stare at her. I looked at her for three reasons:

(1) her face was twisted in contemplation;
. (2) she was wearing a beige kurta with a
transparent golden dupatta; and
(3) she was fucking gorgeous.

I am a woman who takes great pleasure in noticing other women, in raw appreciation for our sex, but also as a comparative study. I could not, however, take the time to assess her beauty. She was onto something strange.

Her head darted behind and to the side; I was sure she was checking to see if anyone was looking at her. She was in the center of a vast bamboo garden. No one else was around. I was in the corner, out of her view. She looked back to the center, her facial muscles tweaked with confidence. She took a few deep breaths and started to tremble. I saw a man—white shirt, beige pants, thick hair—walking toward her. Suddenly, she began shaking violently, falling off the bench, saliva pouring out from her mouth. As she fell, the man broke into a trot and I found myself jogging toward her too.

"Don't put anything into her mouth, let her be," he said firmly before I even reached them.

I froze, holding my hands up in the air. He kneeled beside her and soothed her with his voice. "It's going to be over soon, Sara. You've got this. It's going to be over soon."

She seemed to stabilize:, her body stilled, her face relaxed. He scooped her up, pushed her hand back, took her dupatta dupatta and wiped her mouth. Then he looked at me.

"Thank you for your concern, she has seizures sometimes."

A man had never appeared so authentic to me. It made my heart flare up with an unseasoned emotion, a longing to hold his hand. Perhaps his authenticity was all the more palpable because of the inauthenticity of her seizure. None of it, I was beginning to realize, seemed real.

"Hey, I'm okay," the woman croaked. She stroked the man's face and looked toward me. "This is so embarrassing." She sat up almost athletically and recrossed her legs on the bench. "I am Sara, and you are?"

"Mira. Do you need to go to a hospital?"

"No, she just needs to get back to her medication," the man said with a hint of irritation, a dash of affection.

"I hate taking it every day. If you saw my med routine you'd think I was eighty-four, not twenty-nine."

His name was Rahil and Sara was his wife. They'd been married seven years and had met in college. They didn't seem shy, but I felt that there were only a certain number of questions they would answer, so I stopped. For a second or two there was silence. We heard a bird coo; we heard the feet of other walkers shuffle behind us. Rahil sat down by me on the mud, craning our heads to look up to Sara. Rahil reached toward me and dusted speckles of mud from my sneakers. I couldn't remember the last time someone had touched me with absentminded affection. Sara looked down at my sneakers. "I love the blue laces."

"Cool," Rahil confirmed, as he pulled one of my laces out and then proceeded to tie it back. I wanted to giggle. A grown man and woman amused with my sneakers in the middle of a park. A couple willing to Sunday socialize minutes after a medical emergency. I looked at Sara, trying to discern what had happened. Was she really okay? Why didn't she want to go to a hospital? And had she in fact started her seizure only after she'd made sure Rahil had appeared in the park?

Sara put her hand on Rahil's head, ruffled his thick black hair, and asked him for some water. He pulled out an orange bottle from his backpack and handed it over.

From her purse she pulled out a card of pills trapped in plastic bubbles. She popped a couple out of the foil, flipped them in her mouth, took a swig of water, and then immediately turned to me.

"So what do you do?"

It was one of those questions I couldn't begin to answer. It was also one that had a very simple answer. "I teach English, at Seven Seeds."

"International School?" Sara asked. Her mouth moved like she was tasting the ghost of the pills she'd just taken.

"Yeah..." I said. My voice trailed as I saw Rahil looking at me, deeply, endearingly. Sara's eyes were right back on me. She seemed so present in the moment, and it made me uncomfortable.

"We live close by. Come? We rarely have people over." Her voice was syrupy sweet, like an adolescent talking to her bestie in high school.

"But don't you need to go to your doctor? You just lost consciousness."

My question quivered but retained authority. Testing her. Testing myself. Her face didn't flinch. "Oh, but it happens all the time. I know what to do; I just need a change in medication. I will see my doctor tomorrow."

Their house happened to be only a kilometer away from the park. A small independent house on a lane that was dotted with houses as small as theirs and as large as small apartment buildings. In front of the house was a white metal table with matching chairs and pale blue pillows on the seats. Large potted plants surrounded the table, an oasis by the door. I imagined Sara and Rahil sitting there in the evenings, her lean legs propped on his thighs, her hair in a high bun, and cups of chai that sat with them as they talked the evening away. The living room was soothing pale blues and pinks. There were wooden side tables and a warm beige sofa that could seat five people comfortably. I plopped myself down and then awkwardly stood right back up, embarrassed that I'd sat without an invitation.

Sara scrunched her face in amusement. "Make yourself at home, really, please, I am not saying that for the sake of it."

Rahil sat on a thickly cushioned chair opposite me. His khakis were spotless except for one splotch of mud on his left knee. His hair was notably thick and purposefully not cut. Sara sat right next to me, so close I could smell her. Soft, musky, with a hint of what I thought had to be rosewater. Rahil pushed his chair a few inches closer. I felt like prey, with two exotic, magnificent animals gathered around me, sniffing, wanting, hunting.

I succumbed easily. Sara's inquisitiveness was erratic, compelling, and kind, gently probing further with each question: "What kind of childhood did you have?" "Do you like being an English teacher?" "Why did you become a teacher?"

And then that inevitable question shot through her lips. Was I married? My eyes lowered for half a second. I lifted my head in the next second and told them.

"How did you live after your husband died?"

Rahil nudged her only at that question and changed the topic to lunch.

Sara didn't argue, but added, "I couldn't imagine living if Rahil died; I would simply kill myself the same day, absolutely, I would."

Sara ate precisely four times a day. Gluten-free, because one of her doctors was sure she had celiac disease. Breakfast at 8:30 A.M., lunch at 1:30 P.M., a small supper at 5:00 P.M., and dinner at 8:30 P.M. She ate nothing in between and had last eaten candy and chips four years ago. So long, she couldn't remember what they tasted like. Her rigidity in her diet helped her cope, but her body continued to attack her every day: pains in her back and knees, nausea, and seizures. No doctor could put a finger on it.

Sara's eyes lit up only when she was asking questions, or when her health was being discussed. At first this made it hard to keep answering. My self-worth would rise, her interest in my life making me swell with stories. It was the specificity in her questions that would make anyone not just want to answer, but to do so articulately, precisely, vulnerably. But when I answered, the light dimmed and I was met only with a sturdy focus on my gaze, her face blank but composed. I realized I needed her eyes to stay on me. I'd answer anything. Deeply personal things I had never even thought of: *How did I survive Ketan's death? How did I break out of the young widow cliché? How did I manage to work? Where were my scars?*

Emotional pain can be so severe, so profound, so soul breaking, that it must reflect on the body. But I couldn't seem to find my scars when I stood in front of the mirror. Perhaps they disguised themselves, moving across my skin like a flea on a cat. Maybe they were in the hollows where my neck meets my ears, or hidden in the curve of my back. Maybe the pain scarred the smile of my armpit, lurked in the quiver of my chin. It must have been there, coded into my consciousness and embedded into my genetic material, ready to pass on to a child one day.

I looked at Sara. Dark skin, high cheekbones, a small forehead, wide shoulders, tiny hands with sea-blue nail polish. Her breasts were large, her cleavage pushing out of her V-neck blouse. Where did her pain reside? Because it was there—you could feel Sara's pain, it ate at you, chewed your mind as you talked to her and laughed with her. Her pain was unadulterated energy, a ghost that pulled her and the person sitting next to her together. For a whole second, I felt the soul inside my body throb, thudding like a bass speaker at a club. I wanted to gnaw at her skin, stay with her until I inevitably found the purpose of life. This was Sara, from the very first meeting.

Our afternoon wandered into evening. Sara couldn't drink on her medication, but Rahil poured out whisky for the two of us.

I got the sense that Rahil's job was stable and that he was high up in the ranks. He talked about the city and its transitions in his years here, roping in quick nostalgic facts and anecdotes. Occasionally he'd throw an innocuous question at me. Sara would use my answers to ask the more probing follow-ups. At some point it became almost a rhythm in the room: superficial question, answer, probing question. We talked in hushed sentences for no reason, tilting back glasses of liquor, swaying to something old and mystical from Rahil's speakers. Cloistered, safe, but at risk, like it was a night at our neighborhood speakeasy. We ate dinner together. Incredibly delicious leftovers from the fridge. A mild chicken curry with potatoes, brown rice, a cucumber and tomato salad.

"Know what the secret ingredient is?" Sara asked. "My mother never made just regular chopped salad. She always grated ginger and mixed it in."

Rahil looked into his food and repeated the word *ginger* for no reason.

It was six P.M. Tomorrow was Monday, and the amount of work and mundane tasks to come started to magnify and flood my whisky-warmed body. I could have stayed longer. Rahil's body language was neutral, but Sara's had become increasingly fidgety. I made my first motions of leaving after she went into the kitchen to refill her glass of water for the second time. When I started to stand up and walk toward the door, Sara's enthusiasm rose again, sending an odd burst of hope through my gut.

"You have the whole week ahead of you, but we all just had such a connection, we have to meet again," Sara said. The thrill in her voice was familiar. That thrill that comes when you know you're only minutes away from being able to retreat into your private space again. The relief that comes from knowing you're done with the forced smiles and small talk that prolonged social engagement demands. Still, she hugged me earnestly, and I spent most of my hug inhaling her. Rahil gave me a quick side-hug and then stood by the door with his hands in his pockets. They didn't walk me out to the gate, but they stood at the doorway, staring me out.

That night, when I was alone and in my bed, I thought about Sara's face, its stillness when she listened to my answers. Yes, her face was calm, but it was also accepting, a scientist taking notes on her increasingly willing subject. I'd had enough of an instinct for self-preservation so as not to tell her everything, of course. The closest I came was admitting that my teaching job was a way of changing the way I had lived. It hadn't originated from ambition or any real passion to teach.

I brought my pillow closer to my body and thought of her mouth puckered ever so slightly. Again, I thought of her on the park bench, glancing around before starting to convulse. What had her face looked like before she started to shake? I could picture it only if I closed my eyes and re-created her in my head. I was filled with Sara the whole night.

Then at 1:20 A.M. my cell phone rang. It was Rahil.

"Listen, Mira, she doesn't know I am calling you right now, but I need to talk to you."

II

Did I promise to tell you this story chronologically? Yes, I did. But I must make room for the distractions of my past. It's not an unfair move on my part; ask yourself, don't you carry pieces of your past with you every day? It manifests as fear when standing in a small elevator, and sometimes it holds your tongue and warns it into submission. But the other parts, they come in the form of memory, mostly for no rhyme or reason.

Soon after I met Sara and Rahil, I started to think of my mother several times a day. A melancholic mother, she was, but there was no classical romanticism about her, at least when it came to her depression: she wasn't beautiful enough.

The world loves a beautiful depressed woman. Long hair tumbling over slumped shoulders. Wasting beauties locked in bedrooms, their combs trembling through knots in their hair as they stare listlessly into the mirror. These women possess hips that never threaten the seams of their cotton pants. These women smell of old musk, or the faint scent of a closet in a summer home. Not my mother. She wasn't ugly; she was only plain, and it is far more difficult to be plain than ugly. At least that's what she used to say. Being plain meant you were assured some of the things good-looking people had, but not everything. Being plain allowed you to know that certain things were off-limits. But if you were ugly, you knew exactly how to build your world. And if you were fierce enough, you would end up building a vibrant one, because you knew better. That's what she said, my mother.

A couple of years ago I read about tuberculosis in the Victorian era. Tuberculosis and feminine beauty became interchangeable. For decades the beauty industry made its money off the tuberculosis look. Any lotion or blush was manufactured to flush the cheeks that certain shade of pink that imitated the reddening of skin caused by frequent fever. Then the corsets came and sucked their bellies in. If you could waste away with grace, there was no misery in your existence.

My mother would not have inspired the Victorians.

Her face was full, arms freckled, hair thick, lips in a perpetual pout, and body resigned. She loved me fiercely, but there were days I didn't exchange a word with her, because she preferred to walk about the house, her face almost exquisitely blank. You couldn't bear to interrupt it with the everyday. I found ways to occupy myself, reading factoids in encyclopedias and quizzing myself on scraps of old stationery. Awarding myself stars and smiley faces. I was okay being a loner. I was enamored of her mystery and her waves of isolation. My mother reminded me of my future.

I must have been twelve or thirteen, when she came to my room. Her face had spread into a welcoming smile.

It made me feel dizzy, even though I was just sitting on the bed. She came and sat right next to me. I'll never forget the green cotton sari she wore, the curls in her frizzy hair, the thin gold bangles on her thick wrists. "How are you doing, Mir-Mir?"

I remember shrugging my shoulders, caught off guard. And I remember feeling cheated, resentful that I hadn't been given enough time to prepare for this one spectacular moment: my mother sitting by me, cooing in my ear, asking me how I was. I had stuck my hand out to her awkwardly, but my voice came out steady.

"Ma, how come you look so sad most of the time?"

And my mother had looked at me, squeezed my bony shoulders, and whispered into my ear:

"There is a need for every emotion."

"What is it, Rahil? Everything okay?" I couldn't shake the feeling that Sara was listening on another line.

"No, it's just that I need to talk to you about Sara. She hasn't ever had a friend. Ever since she got... you know." He inhaled. He exhaled. "Sick."

I wanted to ask him then: What is *really* wrong with her? My mouth clenched in restraint instead. "I haven't been able to talk to anyone like a friend in so long either. I mean, no social life. I am not complaining but...you know."

"I know what you mean," Rahil said, his words barely audible.

I promised to return to their house the following weekend. I put the phone down with conviction. I dropped my face into my pillow and slept dreamlessly. Tomorrow, I'd be back to the ordinariness of my life.

A Preamble to My Everyday Teaching Job

Perhaps I glorified the French intellectual movement a tad too much. The school certainly thought so, warning me to tone down my syllabus dodging. Parents had called me too, weeping, enraged, in awe, that their children were talking—much too much!—about communism and philosophers. Name-dropping terms like *utilitarianism*! But I always mediated such complaints with a certain brand of nonchalance that, more often than not, left my accusers morally unsure of their own understanding of the world. I created enough uncertainty that they ultimately gave me the benefit of that doubt.

At the end of the day I was, in fact, a teacher. I taught the English syllabus well enough to the ninth-, tenth-, and eleventh-grade students at Seven Seeds International. Some people mistook me for being an instigator of sorts. Some kind of Emmeline Pankhurst. But I wasn't. I was meeker than that. I was just obsessed with certain time periods, and I made my students obsessed with them too.

Simone de Beauvoir's *The Ethics of Ambiguity*, for example, was mandatory reading for my tenth and eleventh graders. I was obsessed with de Beauvoir because she, like most women, had a knack for simplifying the complexities that men create for the sake of their egos. She boiled the words spun by men down to an accessible existentialism. Most of my students did not bother to read her, but the few who did would come to me crying afterward. The things they'd felt before now seemed only truer, they would tell me. The world was too absurd, too heavy to have any relevance. And we would talk about it until everyone was satisfied with something more wholesome and candid. Gandhi's "Whatever you do will be insignificant, but it is very important that you do it" usually satisfied them in the end.

You might think it was teaching that saved me from the blunt darkness that comes with the loss of a spouse. It was not. I almost committed suicide, true, but it was Camus, Sartre, Foucault, and de Beauvoir who led me back to life. These philosophers who embraced the absurd made my pain feel silly. It made the world seem indulgent and, most of all, purposeless. I followed the wisdom of these postwar intellectuals with an addict's desperation. My everyday in smoggy, stifling Suryam was a very different reality from the European past I conjured in my head: the winter crisp and the woolen coats clenching the chests of these writers. Then I'd look at the bare cotton kurta I wore. I felt the whimsy and entitlement of the cows stoically chewing their cud as they sat in the middle of major intersections. I wanted to laugh at it all, all our perceptions of existence, all our grand ideas of hope and reality. And this, somehow, saved me.

All I know now is that I am still alive, and I find grief bothersome.

When I went to Rahil and Sara's house the next weekend, Rahil wasn't there. Sara said he'd be back in an hour or so and ushered me into her bedroom.

It was a messy room, but still clean. Everything smelled freshly laundered, her sheets radiating with essential oil. Sara's face seemed thinner since the last week, but more beautiful. Her eyes were shining and her hair was tied back. Her lips bloomed from her bare face, plump, puckered, present. She patted the side of the bed and gestured for me to sit down beside her.

"I've been exhausted this week, I have no idea why. It's like I could stay in bed forever. But then I feel sharp needles in my head, an ache really, I have no idea, I just stare at the wall."

"The Yellow Wall."

"Huh?"

I couldn't help the involuntary pride that warmed my cheeks as I savored her confusion. I know I've read far more than most of my peers, but with Sara it was a win. My knowledge was a knife that could cut the thickness of her mystery, if only for a second.

"Oh, nothing, you know men used to like to keep their women in bed—they called it hysteria."

"You're so smart, Mira, really you are, but you see, I know about mental illness. It's a physical sickness, what I have, and it's causing me to shut down."

I moved my hand to her shoulder in solidarity, but she brushed it off dismissively.

"No. No more pity about me, forget about me, tell me all about your love with Ketan, you only talked of his death last time."

No mental safety valve was employed in my response to Sara. It was something I had never done with the discipline it required. This was the moment.

Ketan and I (A Succinct Version)

Let me confirm one thing now, because it's simply true. Love is only romantic when you've lost it. Or if you can't have it. In the end, I lost my love. Eventually, the pain and vulnerability and howling grief were drowned in the bitterness and the boredom that only insomnia can birth. But was Ketan a "love" before he died?

Kierkegaard, the Danish philosopher, said romantic love and marriage could never be experienced in the same lifetime. This is why we humans perpetually suffer from angst, or rather a running between two conflicts, an oxymoron, two things that can never be at once. Heart-break arises only when you've been stupid enough to expect anything as a given: a happy marriage that lasts fifty years, children who grow up and don't die before you, or a promotion that comes every few years. Heart-break only comes from expectation.

I had a naive, awkward, gentle expectation of Ketan. That he would be with me until I was old. That I would probably be the first to die. That he, if anyone, could bear the brunt of losing me.

Mundane office love stories are the most predictable of all. They only exist because people like us forget how to express our desire to live and love beyond the walls of conference rooms and meetings where glances can be exchanged. Ketan and I were the sort of people who thought social bonding was employing a chai break to talk about a coworker with smug judgments. Our moments of joy were heaped upon the everyday baseline of light traffic, three-day weekends, and the candied HR emails that urged us to keep leading and achieving our "goals."

He was a project manager. I was leading internal communications. I've forgotten the main purpose of the company we used to work for. There were far too many experts, far too many divisions, for anyone to form a cohesive image of the entire company and its place in the world. I barely had an idea then, much less now. Still, I controlled its intranet, sent out firm-wide updates, and helped the interns resize images. Maybe it's precisely being such a cog in the machine that allows you to fall in love in the first place. If you are trapped in mundanity, it's impossible not to latch your poor soul to something, or someone, that makes you realize your vulnerable pumping heart will only beat a certain number of times. No matter how clean the air is inside those air-conditioned walls.

Ketan carried himself with a gentleness I'd seen in no other man. He had a beard, five years ahead of the trend, and a make-you-believe-in-God smile. Yes, the fucking charming smile cliché. Expectations, after all, are made of clichés.

I developed a crush on him his first day in the office, at which time I'd already been at the company for a year. I came up to him with an unnecessary and largely irrelevant question. He never called me out on it and was quick to find some kind of legitimate office connection to justify us loitering by each other's cubicle most of the day.

We both came from conservative enough families, but we were no prudes. We took off to Pondicherry the first three-day weekend we got. We went to French cafés, grabbed beers, and ate spicy seafood by the beach. We got right down to sex in the hotel, no qualms, though he was my first. I never asked if I was his. I assumed I was. He made love by searching. Searching for something through the act. You could feel his confusion, his need to express something, something locked in by his body. In exchange I made love by letting him find his own answers. I stroked his hair, whispered into his ears, easing his anxiety. One morning, he lay on the bed after sex. He rubbed his beard and grinned. The grin disappeared and his mouth puckered in thought.

"It's like I have so much more to do."

Then he got up, went to the bathroom, came out and asked me if I wanted to explore Auroville. We got married eight months later in a simple ceremony. His parents, my father, our friends, and a majority of our office coworkers were present. We bought a three-bedroom flat twenty minutes from our office. Ketan said that it wouldn't be long until it took forty minutes to get there. *We're crawling all over this city, multiplying like insects, aren't we?* he said.

So far, all our expectations were alive and well. Our workdays, our lunches, and our dinners together. Our friends on the weekends, our lovemaking at night. Such basic expectations.

Seven months later he died in a really stupidly common accident. At a spot equidistant from the house and our office. It was a two-wheeler accident. A two-wheeler, not because we couldn't afford a stupid car, but because it was the faster way to move through the city. And his helmet was shit and it cracked. Still, nothing had happened to his head. His middle section was run over, resulting in massive internal bleeding. What a bunch of shit the body is made of. It's put here on earth to take emotional bullets all day and night, but one thud, a bit of force, and the body immediately gives up. Bleeding, bursting, rendering itself so fucking useless. When I was brought to the morgue to see him, I had only anger and disgust for the human body. What a horrific joke, what a silly, stretchy, fragile, untrustworthy thing it was. I started screaming. I pounded his chest, his fucking stupid bleeding-ass stomach that couldn't seem to have gotten its act together in time. I smacked his face, I screeched, *You fucking idiot, get up, why are you so fucking weak?*

I never got to see his cremation. My father had me drugged and kept in a hospital room, lurching in and out of consciousness for a week. Each time I woke up, my father would come up to me and coo soothing words that jumbled together. He kept telling me to rest. Friends came in; they talked to me like I was a geriatric patient with Alzheimer's. Like I had no idea what had happened, when in fact I could remember every little insult I had screamed, every little word I'd said to Ketan's dead body. My anger was only artificially tamed. I could feel my body being medicated, like a hot water bag on top of a raging, crampy, menstrual tummy. I wanted to laugh at the doctors and their medication—what fucking idiots, like I didn't know what was there. Like I couldn't feel what was inside of me. I just couldn't act on it, because my lids fell, then they stretched across my face and covered my entire body, like cling wrap. I was a butterfly in a cocoon, a cocoon made out of my eyelids, and it felt damn good.

Later, I was put in a recovery home for six months. Where we had collective goals, where we talked to warm, self-aware therapists. Appa called it the farm. I ate upma every morning and drank mosambi juice every evening. It's also where I read Sartre's *Nausea*, and Kafka, and about feminism, the Enlightenment, and everything in between. I soaked it up, thriving in privileged absurdity and philosophy. I still have no idea why a humble recovery home offered such a wide array of European enlightenment and existentialism, stacked shelf upon shelf. It seemed like an inside joke by the founder of the place (who was dead and whose children had promptly sold it off to a private company).

Like most important European men, I too found myself in exile. And like them, I would survive. I would obey Albert Camus and honor the freedom I had every day. It worked. One day, about six months after my arrival, I felt so free that I saw the innate absurdity of authority crumbling at my feet. I went to the office and told them that I was free. They said I was 110 kilometers from the city and that I'd need to contact my father. I told them I was twenty-nine years old and I couldn't possibly need my father's permission.

They said they could offer no transportation. I had no phone. Only theirs. *I'll walk home*, I told them. They only nodded their heads; they didn't believe me. So I walked righteously toward the gate, where a scrawny watchman saw me coming. He very methodically checked the latch on the gate. I told him to let me out. He only said, *Madam, no, madam, no.* So I walked up to the gate and unlatched it. I was kind of surprised that the guard made no other attempt to stop me from leaving the farm; he just stood there frozen to the side, looking past me as I walked toward the highway. I guess when someone sees a person who's truly embraced her freedom, one can only be stunned into a fleeting, temporary realization of one's own invisible chains. Don't you think?

III

Sara had barely spoken. She took in every word and savored every lengthy monologue. Every muscle of her face worked to engage with me. The semi-clench of her cheeks, her tilted head, and her puckered lips. Every micro-reaction was for me. It was only at the end that I told her it was my first time. I had never summarized that year for anybody, there had just been fragments of my past that lurked and danced between my ribs.

"You aren't alone anymore, Mira."

"That too would be a foolish expectation."

"Why, because I am so sickly I could die at any moment?" She laughed hysterically, her entire body jostling on the soft bed.

She stopped smiling abruptly, took my hand, and leaned forward. I smelled musky, rosy talcum. My eyes moved, helplessly, to her spilling cleavage. There were tiny, squiggly, fading stretch marks traveling around her breasts, ending before they reached the collarbone. She palmed my cheeks, then looked me in the eyes. I wanted to kiss her right then, but I knew it would toss my entire world up in a second. So instead I asked a question that was more intimate than a kiss.

"What makes you so sick?"

Her eyes winced and she snapped her body away. There was a moment of static silence and I panicked. Then she exhaled slowly. Within seconds she had recomposed herself.

"I've always been sickly, Mira."

Her life, she said, was surrounded by tests and medical visits, homebound restrictions and dietary experiments. The thing was, though, that one problem fueled a solution and that solution created a new problem.

"Our bodies are like the world, Mira: beautiful, hysterical, hypocritical, mysterious, poor, and temporary. Mine just happens to be all of those at once."

Rahil, she said, was fatigued by the hospital trips but he never complained. Would I come with her for a new series of blood tests? Pulling her hair up in a bun, she explained that she needed to talk to her neurologist about changing her seizure medication. Her voice grew thick with purpose and excited focus as she described the medication she had been on and how it needed to be adjusted. I looked at Sara's body. She was thin, but her chest created that illusion of health. Her breasts remained full and wholesome even if all she wore was a baggy white kurta. I wanted to imitate Sara's style. Her whites, pale blues, and pastel pinks. Her loose, delicately embroidered tunics and kurtas, and most of all her perfect cotton pajamas she wore underneath. Those cotton pants always hit her ankles perfectly. I knew I could never do it, though, because it would be too obvious I was trying to look like her. I had always been a functional woman, finding the most convenient things capitalism had to sell me: jeans, T-shirts, boring digitally printed kurtas, and the occasional skirt.

I agreed to go with her to the appointment. Then I asked if I could make some tea in her kitchen. Sara instructed me to make chamomile. "Make a cup for Rahil too, he will be here in a minute, he just texted."

My heart thumped and I felt the rise of guilt float up my throat—Rahil's secret call with me, Sara's intimate closeness with me. Two magnets, but Sara's was stronger.

Their kitchen was modest but pretty, with a certain feminine delicacy. More pale blues, like the clothes she wore, and grapefruit reds. Everything was thoughtfully placed: a lavender-and-blue hand towel tucked by the stove, a kettle on the shelf, glasses and pale cream bowls stacked right next to blue-and-white plates. They had Kamala come in every day at 5:00 A.M. and finish by 7:45 A.M. I had never seen her, but she washed the dishes (whatever little Sara could stand to leave in the sink), swept the floors, and took at least twenty-five minutes to dust and replace all the teacups and boxes of spices on the shelves. Up until a month ago I had my Mona, middle-aged and chatty, coming promptly at 5:00 P.M. to clean. Mona even offered to cook because she felt sorry about my life. Over the months her kindness turned into pity, and I found myself withdrawing into my room for privacy as she listed out the reasons I needed to remarry. When she said she was going to move to Delhi because her son was doing well there, I was relieved. I hadn't bothered to look for a replacement; I kept my house in fair shape on my own, save for a layer of dust that coated my lampshades and shelves, even though I tried to dust the house every three days. "How American," Sara had remarked, but she seemed impressed.

I found an airtight glass bottle with whole yellow chamomile flowers on the shelf right next to the kettle. I took out a couple, crushed them between my fingers and smelled them.

When I was fourteen, my father had a huge fight with my mother over chamomile. The crux of it was how expensive whole chamomile was and how ludicrously posh it looked in our middle-class home tucked in a little bottle among fresh ground spices and roasted millets. My mother said it settled her nerves, having gotten a taste for it from her old school friend who'd brought her some from America. After that my mother bought a packet every week from a tea boutique in the center of the city. It went on for almost a year, until that morning, when my father flung the bottle onto the floor. My mother looked stoically at the mess and walked up to her bedroom. I could hear her sobbing all afternoon.

I've never understood how some children get so upset about their parents screaming at each other. I would have given anything to have grown up with two sure individuals who articulated (with violence or anger or just goddamn clarity) what they wanted. But no, my mother sobbed, my mother would not give you a response in the moment. She would hide, and you would hear her ghostly sobs and feel her utter confusion of the world. And my father, who was truly no monster, would feel terrible but not have the courage to console her. So he would walk out, do God knows what, and come back hours later when everybody was back to an everyday joyless but life-affirming task, like making dinner, or doing homework, or sewing buttons onto a school uniform.

Chamomile and my mother. And now it came back years later with Sara. I saw no irony in it. I inhaled the smell of the kitchen, feeling only comfort and security. By the time the water was hot, Rahil was behind me with his finger on his mouth. He was wearing a white linen shirt, glasses, shaggy hair tossed all over. Looking overqualified in general.

"Listen, sorry I'm late, we'll meet alone next time so I can tell you some stuff, but, um, I am going to her room now—see you there." Rahil had the ability to turn something uncomfortable into something thrilling.

I filled cups with hot water and added an individual tea steeper to each of the pale cups. I brought the tray into the room. At once, Sara and Rahil looked up to me with expectant smiles. That moment was filled with such joy that it pushed against my chest and made me want to inexplicably crumble to my knees and sob with gratitude. Some moments can do that to you.

The One Intimate Thing
Ketan Told Me Before He Died

Most love stories glorify the extraordinary secrets shared and life bonds made between couples when they fall in love. The truth is couples mostly fall in love because of some very boring parameters: similar experiences and access to the resources that result in life experiences. Class, in other words. The very foundation of the arranged marriage, which takes similarity so seriously that—barring only directly shared DNA—it requires nearly everything to be the same. The food you eat, the people you know, the places you socialize, the specific gods you pray to—all the same. You hardly have a chance to be surprised by your partner. In Indian tradition, it is considered wise *not* to be unnecessarily surprised. Go with the plan that's been drawn for you and make the most of it.

It's not like a romantic marriage is much different. Sure, the gods Ketan's family prayed to were different, and they raised him vegetarian (a practice discarded the moment he was in college). We didn't possess the exact same background to gird our foundation, but we were similar enough to dance to the tune of happy urban complacency. And apart from the goofy impressions we made of our coworkers, we didn't have any secrets to share or keep. None of that. Except for one time, when Ketan told me a story about his childhood, a story that was uncharacteristic of him, not only in the fact of its telling, but in the story itself.

It was burdened with complexity, mystery, and a certain sense of ambiguity, as if he was searching for the answer from me. He told me this story three months before he died. We were lying in bed and had just shared a bottle of cheap Indian wine. We were taking turns finishing a bottle of water in order to hydrate before sleep. The story goes something like this:

When Ketan was nine, he lived in the north of India in a small industrial town. He had no friends, because his family had just moved there temporarily from Agra, plus Ketan was very shy. They had landed there in the summer, so school hadn't started yet, and he was left to his own devices for most of the day. In the afternoons, when it was brain-damage hot, he would leave his house with a thick cloth wrapped around his head and walk the edges of the town. I have no idea why his parents allowed him out in the heat like that, but as Ketan summarized it, "it was just that time and those kind of parents." One day, he saw a small pathway. The road had cracked and it was mostly muddy. It led to wild trees and bushes. He said he immediately recognized the pathway and set upon it confidently.

"Like a past-life kind of thing?" I'd giggled, but he ignored me.

Young Ketan was certain he would find a well at the end of the path. He was right, but the well was not functional like he expected, nor was there a lush tree shading it. He ran up to its crumbling edge and sat on the hot stones. Then he had a vision of the future: He was sixteen, dark, with hairy legs. He wore a dhoti and a cotton shirt, and was helping a group of older men drag out a young woman who had jumped into the well because of a failed love affair. The girl survived, and they eventually fell in love.

He had other visions at the well: His mother, who looked twice her age, by a burning chulha, cooking daal. A dead father. Him embracing the girl from the well.

"Was it sexual?"

"I was a nine-year-old kid when I had these visions, so I couldn't define it—all I felt was a strong love for this girl and it frightened me, because I didn't know what love was."

The girl was older, much older, and Ketan remember-ed himself being slapped by his mother and then smugly given the news that her family had killed the girl—an honor killing kind of thing. Ketan figured out the honor killing bit only when he got older and could contextual-ize his memory of the vision with the harsh realities of Indian life.

Then the visions stopped and nine-year-old Ketan sobbed by the well.

"Then, Mira, I felt a sudden need to do something, it was like this purpose, like this fucking purpose, I had never felt such purpose. I am thirty-two today, but the need to live for something was never as strong as it was in that moment."

"Maybe because you're already living your purpose?" I had said it with a sudden insecure need for validation. When you're stupidly living life on expectations, inse-curity will raise its head every chance it gets. I wanted him to say that he had found his purpose, that it had been me. Perhaps I was the honor-killed lass reincarnat-ed so we could live our lives together like we were des-tined to. But Ketan didn't say that, and I didn't provoke the words I wanted to hear. Instead I stroked his hair till three A.M., his last answer circling, crashing into my brain over and over again.

"No, Mir, not even close. I am so far away from it that I might as well die right now."

IV

On Tuesday, I visited my father. Always a practical man, he asked me first about my dietary habits. Was I eating enough protein? He showed me his blood tests. Appa was proud of his self-cure for diabetes. He was a walking campaign for the golden sixties (or sixty-five being the new forty). He had given up white rice, meat, and sweets and relied on whole wheat roti; fresh, lightly spiced vegetables; and plenty of daal. "It's a misconception that you need meat for protein. Nowadays, the meat we eat holds the fear and anguish of the animals; give it up and you will feel fearless."

My father used to eat every animal available to him, in spite of the fact that he grew up in a strictly pious vegetarian Brahmin family. He had turned soft in the last decade, slowly becoming the poster child for PETA. "And sprouts, they have so much protein, more than chicken, so why not start your morning with it, Mira? With some lemon juice..."

I knew that when Appa talked nutrition, it was his way of expressing love. He was didactic only when it came to food. Surprisingly, he never hopped on the "get married again" train, enjoying the independence I exuded.

In fact, it was he who told me to move out and start life in a new place. Relatives were aghast; they had wanted me to move back in with my father as soon as Ketan died. There seemed to be no alternative in their minds: my job was in the same city, my husband was dead, and my father was a widower. One of my gossipmonger aunts even told my cousins that my father probably was having an affair—the only reasonable explanation for wanting me out of the house. But this was untrue, not because I could give you evidence, but because I knew Appa at his very core. I knew he liked a certain kind of predictability. He woke up at 6:00 A.M., walked in the park for an hour, and read the paper on the bench there for another. Appa's cook made breakfast by 8:30 A.M. He hung around with two of his recently retired friends playing rummy in the afternoons and volunteered as the head of the community in his area, coming up with new ways to separate garbage, finding acceptable places for the community to feed the stray dogs, and maintaining the area park. He ate dinner at 8:00 P.M., took a night stroll, scrolled the internet before bed, and went to sleep at 10:30 P.M. He had enough money to last him decades, and he didn't live life extravagantly. Ketan and I used to send him twenty thousand rupees every month, not because he needed it but because it was the responsible thing to do, but he refused to keep the money for himself. Instead Appa had put it in a savings fund for Ketan and me to break into in twenty years, when our future children would go to college.

I learned the joy of predictability from my father, taking refuge in the comfort of schedule, the happy sigh I let out when I reached my bed at 8:45 every night and settled in to read a book, or watch a documentary on unsolved mysteries or World War II. I woke up early too, like all teachers. I ate at 7:30 in the morning, my lunch was cooked the night before and kept ready for me to take to school. Rice and chicken curry, roti and vegetables, or sometimes a tomato and cheese sandwich. I'd be in school from 8:30 to 4:30. I'd teach five English classes—two ninth grades and three tenth and eleventh.

After I escaped the farm, I had lived with Appa for two months. The overwhelming majority of that time was spent convincing Appa that I was ready to start a new life. I didn't convince him with words. It was in the steadiness with which I served him coffee. I mastered his preferred ratio (one-third of his steel tumbler filled with coffee decoction and the rest frothy milk). I looked intently into my laptop in the evenings, squinting my eyes when he passed by to indicate that I was reading something important. My voice didn't crack anymore; I talked to him about Ketan in measured sentences. For Appa, I was in grief's fifth and final stage: acceptance. The truth was I had no idea what stage I was in at all. I felt numb and bored. There were evenings when we'd watch old Tamil movies together while shoveling down mouthfuls of curd rice with mango pickle. There were afternoons when Appa took me to coffee shops and we spent hours reading books and sipping lattes. By the second month I had even joined his residential welfare meetings, nodding my head at neighborhood gossip and getting as riled up as anyone else there about the pothole on Twenty-Third and Main that had still not been filled. So when I told Appa I had applied for a teaching job he showed no signs of worry. And after my year of intensive reading, I felt made to teach.

The principal at Seven Seeds, Mr. Khan, was impressed. Burdened by ideals and knowledge, he was one of those men who felt himself caught up in the strange contradictions of our times—an intellectual man who still had to lead an international school, which mimicked the financial goals of any other for-profit company in "New India." He wore his extra ten kilograms well and dressed like he belonged in academia. Being an international school, there were mandates for teachers to have certain credentials. But Mr. Khan was a self-confessed freethinker. "A real teacher teaches you about life," he told me with a sturdy grin.

The Aristotelian method was his go-to. No one really is the master, all of us teach each other, that sort of thing. We discussed books, of course, and he was disappointed to learn I had been obsessed only with Western literature and philosophy. "When India is the heart of spiritual thinking, and our regional languages have already written about everything these Western men have said, you rely on the West? Although I will say, contemporary Indian English fiction is shit, and India has yet to create its first Kafka."

He had cupped his long gray-splattered beard thoughtfully. "But the point is you read, and you can think for yourself, that's what we need: a teacher who can tell these kids to think for themselves instead of being autotuned robots."

The old me would have shriveled away in fear. I had never thought of myself as an intellectual before. But the books, the months at the farm, the grief, all of it had re-shuffled me at a cellular level. I soaked it in; I felt purpose and ambition burn at the center of my gut.

I didn't promise Mr. Khan anything. I told him my father was a big reader, well versed in history. But his earnestness pushed me closer toward transparency. I told him that I hadn't even been much of a reader until the last year.

"So you mean to say you read this much in just a year or so?"

I didn't tell him where or why. There was no way to properly explain how binge-reading philosophy inside a loony bin could change the way one looked at the world. So I simply said I had taken a year off work. I tried to make a joke about it too. "Give me a few more books, I could probably talk at length about Lao-tzu."

Mr. Khan thought I should take on English because it was the subject I could most easily manipulate, with a syllabus I could add my own vision to. "But don't get on too much about communism—the parents will have a fit. They like their kids to know who Marx was, but they like them to reference his beliefs only in their future applications to Stanford and Harvard."

"You look happier now, Mir-Mir."

Appa sat back in his chair, satisfied at his remark. My heart fluttered nervously. I always felt safer when Appa talked about nutrition. I told him it was school, that I was enjoying my classes: "I might even teach a couple of world history classes next month."

"You always were a World War buff, right from childhood, already knowing the alliances and treaties before your friends, but when it comes to the history of our own nation, you know the bare basics. Perhaps you still are obsessed with the stories of white men, but I hope you'll teach your children to look at their own past."

Of course the only reason I was a "buff" of any kind was that Appa constantly told me random historical facts. But I didn't have the heart to tell him that I'd begun to take real solace in history only after my loss.

It Was Appa Who Taught Me About the World Wars

Appa won't remember this, but he's the one who flipped through my history book when I was twelve and read a summary of the World Wars. We hadn't yet gone deep into the nuances at that point in school.

"The Great War, or World War I, can be summed up in one word, Mir-Mir, and that word is *unnecessary*. It's a great way of understanding human nature. Imagine a handful of people who have different ways of supporting each other: obviously some support increasingly goes to one person, jealousy starts, and before you know it you have unhappy people with unarticulated tension, perceived injustices, and frustration."

It was Appa who told me that after World War II, Nehru had sent Japan an elephant (named Indira) to console its empty zoos and bring smiles to the Japanese children. "It was news that made the American papers too, in 1949."

He said it with such pride that as a child I remember somehow coming to the conclusion that it was Appa who had whispered the idea to Nehru. As he grew older, his interests moved closer and closer to the Indian subcontinent. Perhaps his intellectual curiosity was just resting in my DNA for the first few decades of my life. I had always been a good listener, something Appa had mistaken for a sharp memory and an ability to contextualize things in the larger world. I never became a talker, even as my interest in the World Wars rose rapidly in my teens. I always listened to Appa. Appa always had something interesting enough to say. Sometimes when Amma was in bed, I would hear Appa reading to her, usually nonfiction, usually about history, and usually in one monotonous tone. Those moments brought immense comfort to me, both of them in one room, engaged with each other, my mother listening to the words of my father even if she wasn't really paying attention. Those moments of safety let my entire body sigh, filled my head with hope, and brought heat to my cheeks.

Now, I got that same feeling when I thought about Rahil and Sara.

I looked at Appa's light brown hands, blue veins popping out. His skin was oddly translucent. He was a sturdy and fit man, though. Sometimes I wanted to ask him more about him and Amma, how much he loved her, how much he understood her. Sometimes I wanted to get right to the thick of her and beg Appa to confirm my memories of Amma: silent for days, then perpetually sobbing, then coldly stoic. Amma who I knew had still loved us, she must have. I had actually gotten closer to asking him more about Amma before Ketan died. After his death it got harder. Although Appa saw me more often, the line of emotional questioning was restrained. I wouldn't talk about my time at the farm, and he wouldn't talk about Amma. You know you have the same DNA running through your veins when promises like this can be made without uttering a word.

I opened a package of fried murukku for Appa and placed it on a plate. We drank our coffee and talked about the news. When I was leaving, Appa held my hand and told me to stay happy like this. If it was truly the prospect of teaching history next month that was elevating my mood, then I simply had to continue teaching. "Maybe you'll meet some teacher at school; lots of qualified male teachers these days, no?"

I knew Appa too well to think this was really a nudge to start looking for a new partner. He was just trying to access the true reason I looked happier, in his own unconscious way. When I walked out, I wondered what part of me had lit up...which parts had become so visibly happy.

V

I woke up on Wednesday with a pounding headache. I rarely got headaches, and my tolerance for them was very low. I texted the school admin that I wouldn't be in. Then, like it was natural, I texted Sara.

I have a pounding headache. Can you offer any cures, oh wise one?

I reread my text and immediately regretted sending it. The words implied a long-term closeness and a need for attention. But only thirty seconds later I saw a response.

I have the best pills for that, come here and I'll fix you right up.

Without thinking, I tapped my response. It made no sense, as the reason I had skipped school was so I could rest it out. Yet there I was, pulling a pair of jeans over my hips and throwing on a striped black-and-white blouse. I grabbed my phone, my small embroidered purse, and walked right outside. It was cool, and the Rasagura vendors were out, the fruits stacked one upon the other. I inhaled the tart-sweet scent and found myself walking to one of the carts. An older man stood behind it, a checkered lungi wrapped and pulled up to his bony knees. He was staring into space, lulled by the morning sun. I asked for half a kilogram. He took an inordinately long time to place them on a sheet of newspaper and then wrap them. My irritation faded as I pictured myself offering the fruit to Sara. I saw her eat the fruit in front of me, her eyes twinkling, grateful for my thoughtful snack.

Sara opened the door a full minute after I'd rung the bell. She apologized for taking so much time; her knees were giving her problems. Yes, she was doing the physical therapy, but it was probably because she had eaten something with gluten in it.

"Sometimes Rahil brings packaged food, and we don't always bother checking the labels."

I thought it odd someone as methodical about her health would eat packaged food *accidentally*. Still, I nodded sympathetically and gave her a hug. Musky rose.

"How is your headache?"

On cue my head began to thud again. My hand reached for my left temple and Sara pouted in sympathy. I felt a warm rush spread through my face as she walked toward the living room shelf, pulled open a drawer, and took out a strip of medication. "This will do the trick." She handed me two purple capsules. I didn't ask any questions, but they certainly didn't look like the over-the-counter paracetamol my mother used to rely on. Sara assured me I would feel better in twenty-five minutes and led me to her bedroom, where I was instructed to lie down. Soon, she was caressing my forehead. I closed my eyes. I heard the side drawer open, then shut, then the room came alive with peppermint oil. She rubbed the oil on my temples till they felt like they were on fire, the good kind of fire, the kind that blunted the thudding.

"Tell me about Rahil, you've never talked about your relationship."

My eyes were still closed.

Sara Tells Me How She Met Rahil

Rahil feared cats, which was bizarre because he grew up with them. His mother had four, and various kittens in between, some that stuck around for a year or two, others that died or got run over. Rahil also feared elevators, but he nevertheless took them and skipped the steps at his office. Rahil was essentially a man who lived with his fears. He was twenty years old when he met Sara, who had transferred to his college in Delhi. She was studying history. Rahil was in the third year of his business administration degree. Sara had heard he came from a mixed family too: Muslim mother, Hindu father. Suitably intrigued, she approached him and asked his opinion of the function of religion in mixed marriages. "The function? It's celebrating way too many festivals and holidays, and between the Muslim and Hindu ones, I am pooped."

Sara laughed, but was agitated by his flip answer. Rahil playfully dismissed her as a new age Sufi and called her Rumi for the first four months of their relationship. But he impressed Sara with translations of Arabic poetry, procured through his maternal uncle, a professor in Delhi.

Sara had fragile, protective parents. Even though she was twenty-one years old, she went home at seven P.M., not a minute later. It was a predictability that kept her parents assured of her physical safety and, I suspected, let Sara take refuge in her room, where she listened to music, scribbled in her diary, and then cooked with her mother. Her parents were not opposed to the romance in any way. Rahil was always welcome in their home, an option he ended up availing himself of almost five nights a week, just so he could spend more time with Sara after curfew hours.

They made love for the first time in her room, while her mother and father were out for a Diwali dinner. Rahil was nervous, kept looking at the door and asking what he should say if her parents were to suddenly come home and ask why the door was locked. But Sara calmed him down, convincing him that her parents were more Western that way—too many people in their family lived away from India; she even had a lesbian cousin who had married a French girl in Toronto. Nothing could shock them. If anything, it would be awkward. But Rahil could never reconcile Sara's parents, who were so liberal in thought but so paranoid of Sara doing anything outside the house. "This isn't an American rom-com, Sara," he said.

Their first fight was provoked by Rahil. He had asked if she'd had a sibling who died before. "It must be the reason your parents are so flipping paranoid."

Sara slapped him. For several seconds there was silence. His face was devoid of expression, but Sara's eyes were already welling up with tears.

She claimed it was her own shortcomings—her fear of the world, the knowledge that something was not right within her—that let her parents see her vulnerability. "I could not survive the real world, and my parents know it."

Rahil went back to his old self, holding her, telling her he understood.

One day, a year before they married, Rahil came to her to say that one of Rumi's quotes now made sense to him. Rumi said that once something is cut from its source, that something is always longing to go back. Rahil said he knew that Sara had found the source of real love, of universal divinity. But in coming into this world, one flooded by desire and material things, it was only natural for such a pure soul to want to run away from it all, to return to its source. She was too spiritual for this world, too raw, too pure.

"That's when I knew he had gotten me, and would be the only man to get me, because, Mira, he was like clay; give him enough time, and he will mold himself into something beautiful."

They were married in the winter in Delhi, her mother's hometown. By then Sara had started having symptoms: headaches, joint pain, cramps, hair loss, weight loss, then weight gain, then weight loss again. "And through it all, you know what Rahil always said?" Sara asked me as she applied a few more drops of peppermint oil to my head. I could hear the excitement in her voice.

"'Sara, your soul is rejecting your body, that's all. You want to go back to a place of bliss and love, but I need you, so tell your soul to stay its course, find your Maʿrifa here, find it in this life.'"

Sara stopped rubbing my head. I didn't know how much time had gone by, but I felt compelled to ask where Rahil was, even though I knew the answer. "He's at work, always home at six on the dot."

My headache had vanished. I took in a breath and started to ask Sara the question I wanted to ask the first day I met her. "The seizures..."

I couldn't get myself to say the words: that I had seen her fake it. But was I right? A woman so worldly and spiritual, would she really fake her own seizures?

Sara inhaled deeply and I found myself doing the same. The peppermint in the room had faded and allowed for some of the musky rose to reenter my nostrils. She spoke before I could finish my question: "Since I was twenty-one, when the doctors put me on anti-seizure medication. They are rare, but they do happen. I've been diagnosed with everything, Mira—polycystic ovaries, chronic fatigue syndrome, early-onset arthritis, celiac disease—but really I know there is something much larger at play. I don't even think doctors have a term for it yet."

She had listed off her diagnoses with a building pride, which unsettled me but compelled me to believe her, to believe that there was something very wrong with Sara, something even science couldn't account for.

"Science is one language, Mira. A profound one at that. But just a language. A tree has a way of interpreting the world too, but we can't understand it yet. It doesn't make it any less profound. The mistake we have collectively made is to listen to only one language."

She looked maniacal when she said it. But I couldn't fault her for her view. I imagined Rumi standing in front of her; he would have thought she was the most normal being in this whole city. "That's true" was all I could muster back. She looked at me and shook her head. It was beyond my understanding and that was okay by Sara. I could feel her recognizing my ignorance without judging it, and it made me uncomfortable.

I hadn't texted Rahil back about meeting him alone. I was frightened to take part in something as underhanded as that, but it was now, in Sara's presence, that I felt most compelled to reach out to him. I found myself telling Sara I needed to use the bathroom. Sitting down on the toilet, I started to pee and texted Rahil.

With Sara now, just chatting. Happy to talk with you whenever.

I realized the stupidity of my action midstream. What if he didn't text back immediately, and then I had to read the text in front of Sara, pretending it wasn't from him? I could be deceitful tucked away in the bathroom, but in front of her? I quickly began the work of convincing myself that I wasn't doing anything wrong—I wasn't attracted to Rahil, I wasn't! I was simply reaching out to him. He had the answers to Sara, answers caught between the stories Sara told me, answers to questions I had about Sara but couldn't ask her, because with Sara, you had to wait for a spiritual pause to ask her something intimate. And even then, I sensed, there were certain questions she wouldn't be willing to answer. By the time I was wiggling my jeans up my hips again, I felt my phone vibrate.

Don't text me back. I'll call you late tonight.

The precise instructions let my heart settle back into my chest. I washed my hands and walked back into the bedroom. Sara had propped her back against the bed's wooden headboard.

"Is your headache better?"

"It is, so much better."

"Good, then you won't mind if I ask you why you didn't follow up about coming to the doctor with me. I was kind of hurt."

I sat down, her blunt honesty a rope that had caught my ankle by surprise. "Sara, of course I'll come, I just didn't want to, like, you know, assume that I should have taken charge of it." I tried to compose myself, but my face must have revealed how awkward I felt. An awkwardness that quickly bloomed into excitement. She needed me.

"Are you worried about Rahil? He won't mind, he needs a break."

I told Sara it wasn't about Rahil, but I stumbled through my sentences, my words running into one another. But Sara didn't even blink once. She puckered her lips like a fish and dismissed my faltering. "Whatever, as long as you just come with me this Friday."

Sara opened her side drawer again, pulled out her iPod. Her speakers by her closet poured out Arabic beats. "It's Sufi music, from Turkey," she mumbled. She swayed her hands, occasionally clenching her fingers in and out as she moved her upper body to the music. I sat by her and just watched. Minutes passed—it took seven or eight of them for me to realize that this wasn't a temporary thing. She was in it for the long haul. I closed my eyes and started to sway my body too, tried to feel the music, this Sufi ecstasy that Sara had talked so much about. Humans are truly fucking stupid—we are happy to follow as long as someone else is doing it. We follow no matter how bizarre we might think of the same action independently.

The words were repetitive and there were loud, breathy exhales in the music creating an echo-like beat. I let the flute notes walk into my ear, swirl in my mind, crawl out the other ear, and then loop around my body. I was well aware Sara and I must have looked spectacularly ridiculous on the bed, using half our bodies to dance. But if you do something long enough, repeatedly enough, you start to lose yourself.

I opened my eyes to see the time was five P.M. I had fallen asleep during this trance dancing, the side of my face patterned by a pillow. Next to me, Sara was asleep as well, and I studied her hair. It wasn't black hair, it was a darker brown, but not dark enough to be confused with black. I threw my hand out to her ponytail and gently wrapped a lock of her hair around my index finger. Her hair was soft, but not necessarily glossy.

I guess what I was looking for was some sign of physical failure in her hair, but it was healthy enough. Not Head & Shoulders healthy, but still, it was nice hair. I moved an inch toward her, the faintness of her rosy talcum rushed through my nose once more. It wasn't as powerful this time. Her white kurta had come together against her spine, almost outlining the curve of her back. It's true she didn't act like a healthy person, but was this woman just a liar?

My hands grazed over my phone in my pocket. I wanted to text Rahil again, but knew better. He would be home in less than an hour. I decided to stay. I went to the kitchen to make chamomile tea, knowing it was what Sara would have asked me to do anyway if she was awake. The kettle started to whistle, I heard *thud-thud* from the next room.

"I just remembered I got some fresh Rasagura," I called out. "Can I cut one up for you?"

"Yes," Sara's voice echoed to the kitchen.

I poured the hot water into the cups and added two spoons of dried chamomile into the individual tea steepers. Then I walked to my bag and took out the fruits wrapped in newspaper. I cut the Rasagura fruits into segments of four, every brown seed visible with the creamy yellow bursting out of its pink rind.

On the bed, we arranged our strange picnic: a plate of Rasagura, our cups of chamomile tea, and, from Sara's drawer, a plastic packet of peanut chikki.

"Isn't it weird no one has figured out why they can't grow this fruit anywhere else? It's the alchemy of our soil, that's what it is," Sara said as she munched on her fruit.

I nodded my head, happy she was talking about the fruit. Happy she was enjoying it. I slurped its meat. They've always tasted like mangoes to me, although popular food critics have said there were far too many berry notes to miss. *While far from overpowering, the berry-citrus taste is subtle but present.* I remembered reading that somewhere.

Sara took another section and reached her hand out to me. I froze at first, but then opened my mouth, letting her put the pulp part in my mouth, and she just held the fruit there, urging me to suck the pulp out. She took back the empty skin, raised her index finger at me, and wiped away the juice on the corner of my lips. I wanted to smell her rose musk at that very moment, but my senses had become too accustomed to the environment, I couldn't discern anything except for the bright notes of the fruit. All of a sudden she curled up her knees and winced.

"Cramps," she whimpered.

I stood up immediately and asked her what I could do.

"Nothing, Rahil will be back soon."

And mere seconds later, the front door creaked open, followed by footsteps toward the room. I looked up. Rahil stood there, in khaki pants and a light denim-colored shirt, in his right hand a cloth bag filled with groceries.

"You're sick again, aren't you, Sara?"

Sara chewed her lip and nodded silently. He walked toward her, sat beside her and stroked her hair. They looked at each other knowingly. I saw his eye catch the pink skins of the fruit on the plate.

"You know Rasagura gives you cramps."

I waited for Sara to defend herself, to say it wasn't the fruit at all. Instead she gave him puppy eyes. They didn't need words. He stroked her face and shook his head in mock annoyance. I sat on the corner of the bed, floating to the memory of the flute in that Sufi song. I closed my eyes.

VI

On Thursday I was hurried into a history class because Mrs. Menon had dengue. In these times, it's hard to figure why all organizations don't simply allocate resources for the inevitability of someone getting dengue. I wasn't scheduled to begin subbing until next month, but I was at ease; it was eleventh grade and the faces were familiar: the same class that usually took English with me.

I soon learned that a certain student, Samina, was in the midst of campaigning Mrs. Menon to make personal essays about World War II mandatory. Seven Seeds took pride in allowing its students to make decisions as long as they could win a classroom vote. For Samina, who was not only fairly brilliant, but also extremely pretty and universally popular, her proposals were always voted in with embarrassing ease, regardless of their merits.

As reported to me by the classroom, Mrs. Menon had been trying to push Samina's proposal off, but Samina had insisted, promising she would be the first one to share her essay. The deal she suggested was simple: if the other students didn't like her essay, they didn't have to do the assignment themselves.

Not long after we began an open-book test that Mrs. Menon had left for the class, Samina approached me with a topic for her essay. Her handwriting was chicken scratch, a paragraph wiggled on a piece of lined paper she held in her hand. The topic: Hitler's ambush in Russia in 1941. In fact, the kid wanted to write about the specific consequences of Hitler's disastrous mistake: the utter lack of warm clothes for his troops, resulting in frostbite so bad there were mass amputations and frozen limbs all over the place. That and frozen eyelids, which broke off and fluttered to the ground like shredded meat.

"I want to use the gory details of frostbite as a metaphor for poor leadership and relate it to the leadership examples we have in our country and, for that matter, the world. How all of us are just bodies with their limbs falling off."

Her shiny black hair was tied up in a ponytail and flipped from side to side, as her body reflected the breadth of her feeling, the range of her opinions. Her arms shook, her head bobbed, and her eyes lit up with an intensity I wished I had experienced at her age. This emotional abundance was also her crucial flaw. I wanted to tell her that many feelings weren't worth having, that they destroyed you in the end. But she was going to have to let life prove that to her, not me.

The years to come would blunt her need for metaphors and throw her into the monotony of three-bedroom capitalism. I couldn't let her write the essay; I would almost certainly get in trouble with the parents for allowing disturbing material to be passed around class if I did. And even if the parents didn't create a stir,

Mrs. Menon would take any future opportunity of teaching this class away from me. God forbid I succumbed to dengue—I'd never teach again.

"Samina, you know what I am going to say, you know this topic is wicked awesome," I praised her, a firm believer in integrating contextual vernacular, even as Samina had already started to pout. "But the kind of graphic detail you are going for... Listen, you are only sixteen, and if this were Denmark, no one would give a thought to this being inappropriate, but you know some of the parents here. You don't want this project to go down the drain, so why not get into something acceptably provocative?"

"Like feminism?"

"Like feminism." I smiled. "You could write about the yeomanettes, the first women in the American navy during the war. Starting with Loretta Perfectus Walsh, I am sure you can find a metaphor for our times now, right?"

"Like how the work they did in the navy was largely typographical or nurturing? Or at the very most involved organizing? And how these tasks are still synonymous with women? Like, you know, teaching? No offense."

"I didn't even know what *typographical* meant till I was, like, twenty-eight, but yes, go ahead with that."

"Can I still write the German frostbite one, just for you?"

I rolled my eyes. Only Samina would do extra work for intellectual kicks. "Just don't go around saying it's an official assignment. You want to write about eyelids freezing off, do it on your own time."

Samina went back to her desk, flipped open her textbook, and started working on her open-book test. I took out my phone.

Rahil had messaged the night before, as promised, hours after their strange "sick couple time" in their bedroom. When they were together on that bed, I felt their love, their acute need for each other. Their commitment to their roles was thick, something you were forced to make room for if you were physically near them. Of course, I found it only slightly odd that Sara had winced in pain at 5:59 P.M., but what I found odder was Rahil's ability to know exactly what she needed. His ability to know how she was feeling within seconds of seeing her. Rahil's ability to come right to her, make her the center of his universe, literally, for entire minutes—that's what amazed me.

I increased the brightness of my phone screen and re-read the text.

Weekday afternoon, around 1, what day works?

I couldn't deny the thrill that moved to the surface of my chest. It wasn't like I had unholy feelings for Rahil, but I needed to appear circumspect. Sane enough to be the bearer of his secrets. The secrets of a woman whose scent traveled with me to school, to dinner, and to bed when I slept. I had already taken yesterday off; taking another day would really cramp resources with Mrs. Menon out for the week and two other teachers busy getting engaged and married, respectively.

Next week, Tuesday.

I could come up with an easy excuse to take the second half of the day off, or just pretend there was an emergency on Tuesday before lunch. We texted back and forth a bit more, until I forgot where I was.

"Miss Mira?" It was Abhijit, a mediocre student but gifted guitarist. I felt like an idiot. "Miss Mira, can we go over the Treaty of Versailles again? I don't have enough substance to add to the essay question."

"We can," I said, my head half thinking about Friday and Sara and the inexplicable thrill that was rising now from chest to throat, projecting itself out from my mouth and covering Abhijit, rendering him and the entire class beyond saving.

At lunch, I sat in the staff room looking over my lesson plans for the week. I had essay and grammar worksheets for ninth grade, and for tenth grade we had to discuss the book they were assigned, *The Grass Is Singing* by Doris Lessing. I looked at her name and smiled in excitement: Doris Lessing.

I had spent the night researching more about Sufism, and the more I read, the more overwhelmed I felt. But the raging need to know and to understand that had flooded my mind during my time on the farm failed to make its presence known. I felt like Abhijit, but I needed to be Samina.

I'd found something Lessing had said about Sufism, or rather a great many things she had to say about Sufism. She was interested in the Western obsession with mysticism, juxtaposed with the ecstatic simplicity it really observed. The way she saw it, contemporary Sufism should be practiced openly, without regarding it as any kind of obstruction to other religions.

I wondered if Sara had read Lessing's books, though I doubted it; her knowledge was extensive but narrow, limited to health, nutrition, and her own practice of Sufism. This, of course, was only my preliminary understanding of Sara. What can you tell of another person's intellectual curiosity from everyday conversation? What's the metric by which one can measure real purpose, a sound consciousness, deep perception, via the usual channels of mundane banter? On the surface, things I discussed with Sara were nothing of consequence, but the way our talks made me feel was quite different. The word, if I had to limit it to one, would be *purpose*. I shared purpose with Sara; we were both searching for answers to questions about our lives. Unlike Ketan, we had more time. Maybe Ketan's purpose was to let me find mine. It was a self-centered thought, but the more I considered it, the more true it seemed.

Aristotle, True Friendship, and Sara

Aristotle perhaps defined this well. He believed that good people had in common eleven traits. Traits like courage, truthfulness, magnanimity, and an open, liberal mind. He also believed that in order to make life truly meaningful one had to be in the company of good friends. These friends are not to be mistaken for the people we usually keep company with. They are not the people with whom we make strategic alliances to jump over social hurdles or climb career ladders. They are also not the same people as the friends we hang out with for the sake of good times. In my experience, this type of friendship has been limited to evening drinking, pointless political discussions, and meme sharing. Aristotle prescribed finding true friendships—ones where your concern for a friend's sorrow is all-encompassing, where you meet with purpose, and where you help fill each other's deficits. Friendship of mutual expansion. I think it sounds like what we seek in a lover, but that's the potency of it, the fact that a true friendship must be much more; it must make us all lovers, when exponentially re-created, be able to Band-Aid the entire world and start anew.

Was Sara truthful? I was not sure. Was Sara courageous? Just as quickly I found I was asking myself the same questions. Was I truthful? Was I courageous?

I thought about Rahil. His put-together charm. His sharp jawline and the relaxed-fit pants he wore in an attempt to look older than he was. He needed help and he had asked me for it. There had to be a reason for that, there had to be an answer I carried within me. The last thought I had was most satisfactory.

I grabbed my copy of *The Grass Is Singing* and walked toward the tenth-grade classroom. I heard a group of boys rapping Kanye West. The lyrics were sorely out of rhythm but their voices were shrill and confident. The type of confidence you know is temporary but real in that one moment.

VII

Dr. Mudra tapped his pen on his prescription pad. He was a reserved-looking man with a goatee and mustache. He wore black glasses and, strangely, a bright yellow button-down shirt. On his desk—wide, white, and spotless—was a calendar branded by Alexia, a new antacid.

"Sara, we've discussed this. To control your seizures, and your migraines for that matter, you have to take Toposix, and to be frank, if you don't want to take it, I don't think you are in any danger."

"But what about the side effects, Doctor?"

"You said you didn't have any, didn't you? Some dizziness maybe?"

I shuffled my feet, wanting to interrupt to ask if weight loss was a side effect, because Sara's face had thinned from the first time I had seen her. Instead, I looked at Sara and waited for her to respond. It took at least twenty seconds before she said anything.

"I mean the long-term side effects. I read an article about it wrecking my reproductive system."

"Like I said, you don't have to take them, you know that stress provokes—"

"I know, but what about another MRI scan? Maybe something will appear now, and we can get to a more specific treatment. Toposix is such a generalized medication."

Dr. Mudra sighed, then paused to look at me. His eyes squinted as he tried to guess my role here. He asked Sara if she was the doctor or if he was, to which she laughed girlishly, trying to settle the unease she had created. He opened his laptop and started clicking. "See, you did one eight months ago, and everything was normal. Not all seizure patients show physical signs with an MRI, which is why I have you on the most effective medication."

The appointment rapidly turned awkward. Sara jumped from her seizure issue and asked him about a new treatment (an injection) for her arthritis. Dr. Mudra was visibly offended and told her to see a rheumatologist. After a few breaths, he even wrote a name down for her. He told her to have vitamin B-complex every day and to come back if she had a seizure, at which time he promised to do an MRI again. Sara sat there in defiance, staring back at him. I played with my silver earring, pretended it came off, and spent that minute trying to screw the post back in again with focused diligence.

Dr. Mudra shrugged in defeat. He pulled out Sara's folder again and looked to me for a second, then scanned Sara's blood report from a month ago. "Your blood tests indicated you are slightly vitamin B deficient. If you think the supplements aren't doing it for you, we can do an injection, that usually does the trick."

Sara shrugged her shoulders and said she'd come back if she had another seizure. She stood straight up and walked out without waiting for me. This time my earring fell out for real and clinked on the floor. I hunched down to look for it, feeling Dr. Mudra staring at my back. Glimpsing the shimmer of silver near the corner of the desk, I quickly retrieved my jewelry, nodded awkwardly at Dr. Mudra, and fled.

Sara was infuriated. She was outside, by a poster hanging on the wall that glorified the health benefits of taking the stairs. "See? They always dismiss me, like what is happening to me is not good enough for them. They just want to toss some drugs at me and not do the work, they don't want to figure it out."

She shook her head in disgust, and my heart sunk; she was so helpless before this visit, but now I felt like I was standing next to a stranger. This Sara was empowered, she was entitled, and she was passionate. Her eyes brightened, her body grew rigid; the fragility that once held her captive now fled. She was rock solid and determined.

I grasped her hand—mine wet, Sara's dry—and nodded, trying to be that true Aristotelian friend, letting her anger encompass me. She dug her nails into my palm and I winced, but she didn't notice. We walked out the hospital's main gate. The canteen stood in front, an oasis of happy colors, an escape from the marbled grays and bright well-being blues of the hospital. Sara's hand let go of mine, and she took out her phone and tapped on Uber. She didn't ask me to come with her; she didn't ask me how I would get back. She just said, "Rahil is going to be so pissed. My Uber will be here in a minute."

We waited in silence. Finally, her white car drove up to the passenger pickup, and after getting in she rolled down the window. Her body looked so tiny in the car. Her familiar fragility came back as she tilted her head to the side and looked at me through the half-open window. "Mira, I am so sorry, it's just such a long story, I'll talk to you about it later, promise." Then she waved.

The canteen was full of patients' families and visitors eating samosas and drinking tea. I ordered pineapple juice and a vegetable-cheese sandwich, paid, and received a red token chip to give to the cook. I had my tray in hand when I saw Dr. Mudra briskly walk to my left. He had a glass of sugarcane juice in one hand and his phone in the other. Our eyes met. I was about to avert the situation by turning toward a seat, when he walked up to me.

"Where is Sara?"

I told him she had just left.

"Are you a good friend of hers? She usually comes with her husband."

"Yeah, I mean, she needed someone to go with her."

"You've known her long?"

"Sort of," I lied. The guilt of the lie evaporated as his shoulders came closer to mine.

He nodded thoughtfully. He needed to be goaded more.

"To be honest, Doctor, I think she was angry you weren't taking her seriously."

I wanted to drop my tray and run the moment the words came out of my mouth. I had no idea why I'd said what I had; perhaps her rage was truly my rage.

Dr. Mudra just smiled, nodded his head, and then gently asked me to sit with him. "I want you to know that I take confidentiality very seriously, but I also can't stand to see her suffer like this."

Here was my entrée into Sara's medical world. I took a deep breath and waved my hand over to the empty seats that were right next to us. Then I sat down and looked at him with new interest.

What Dr. Mudra Told Me

Sara had first come to Dr. Mudra three years ago, after her first seizure. She came in with three very organized files and Rahil by her side. He was impressed with her articulate descriptions of her medical history and her warm composure. Her files indicated she had suffered migraines, severe menstrual cramps, constant fatigue, heart palpitations, and joint pain for the last four years. She had been on and off drugs to treat her specific problems along with Ayurvedic alternatives, dietary changes, and even homeopathy. "She's always been anemic, albeit moderately," he said. I immediately felt better; there was something wrong with her! Probably much bigger than anemia, but at least this explained her fatigue, her wasting way—maybe it led to a whole bunch of other issues.

Dr. Mudra took a long pause as he grazed his spoon over his fried vada and chewed his lip. I chanted silently for him to talk, but I didn't want to look overenthusiastic, some trivial quidnunc of a friend.

"What do you think of Americans and their fascination for labeling?" he said finally. "They've labeled every disease in the book, every behavior, every physical ailment. The drug industry has branded its medicine to facilitate specificity. You know, there is a specific medicine unique for every label."

I sipped my pineapple juice, nodded my head. "Usually it is good to know what you have, right?"

My own depression was triggered by Ketan's death. Then, ultimately (according to my doctors), it altered the chemistry in my brain semipermanently, allowing me to sit in a room for sixteen hours straight reading. It allowed me to seek solitude from people and the everyday. It let me think. It let me weep in the afternoons, weeping provoked by the most random of things: the attendant giving me a glass of juice, reading a funny line in a book, looking at my empty bed when I finally moved to my new house. I took medication for a year.

If I'd lived in the Victorian era, I would have been dismissed as a fragile woman who suffered from hysteria because her husband just died. Or if I had lived a century before in my own country, my depression would have been glorified, needed, and aggressively presented to society as that of an ideal grieving wife. Had the words *clinical depression* empowered me? I couldn't remember.

But I didn't say any of this. I just kept nodding.

Dr. Mudra stared back, trying to provoke a more definite answer from me.

"It's a catch-22 situation, if you ask me," I said finally.

To my surprise, he nodded vigorously in response to my cop-out answer. He recrossed his legs, took another sip of his juice. "The thing is, I try not to label my patients, but sometimes, just sometimes, you need to, so that they can actually be put on the path for a cure."

"Do you think she is just too anxious about her health?"

"Her blood tests and scans have always been normal and, well, she's always had trouble with her menstrual cycles... Here's where I'll end the conversation: if you do care for her as a friend, talk to her husband, Rahil. If you ask me, he's the piece of the puzzle most won't acknowledge."

I pushed my drink away from me in an absurd protest. Sara's rage swam through my chest. How dare he start something and then end it this abruptly.

"What's wrong with Rahil? He takes care of her."

Dr. Mudra shook his head.

"Why won't you tell me what's wrong with her? Is she going to die?"

He put his hand on mine to reassure me. "I must go, but do talk to Rahil. I'll take the consequences if he is upset with me for telling you to talk to him, but let's just say I know Rahil well. It's truly in Sara and Rahil's best interest. You look like a smart girl, and it's good to see she has friends."

Dr. Mudra left me sitting with a quarter cup of frothy pineapple juice. For a few minutes my mind was numb, watching a woman in a black burqa try to feed her impatient toddler. She sliced the idli with the edge of her spoon, dunked it in sambhar and pushed it into his mouth. The sambhar spilled orange all over the front of his X-Men T-shirt. The woman dabbed a tissue into a metal tumbler of water and tried to wipe away the mess as the child started to cry. The mother looked at me and smiled. I gave her the most sympathetic smile I could in return and stood up to leave.

Cars, buses, and two-wheelers exploded all over the place. Next to me was a man selling jackfruit from a cart. He had a little sign that announced he took payments through a digital wallet. A black stray dog lay panting under his blue cart. I caught its brown eyes and the dog's tail lazily wagging in response. The man stared at me. "His name is Raja," he said in Hindi, pointing at the dog. I felt compelled to buy his fruit. I got eight pieces of ripe jackfruit on a small piece of newspaper and chewed it until an auto-rickshaw slowed down and asked me where I wanted to go.

The jerky movement of the auto-rickshaw as it weaved around buses and cars was calming. I went back to the day in the park in my head. Sara, gold dupatta, sitting on a bench. Her eyes had darted around, searching. No, not right. She was checking—checking to see if anyone was watching, of that I was sure. Then her face had looked out straight ahead and she began to convulse.

Rahil.

Rahil came running after she started convulsing. Out of nowhere? No, from my left in the park, jogging toward her. Now that I thought of it, his pace of jogging had been absurdly slow, not rushed, but not walking. It wasn't worried, it was—what was it? Sara on the ground, spit frothing; me walking ahead, faster, toward her. She had faked it. There was no denying this.

Rahil. From the left of the park.

I shut my eyes. It came to me. Sara, checking around her, not seeing Rahil, not seeing me, thinking it was okay to start. I re-created the scene again and that's when I saw it. Rahil was there, he hadn't come from nowhere, he was standing diagonally behind her. She had missed him. But he was there. I had just been too distracted by Sara to notice him. I closed my eyes again and remembered. Now I was sure. Rahil was there, he saw her too. He saw her fake her seizure. Rahil saw Sara look around before she started to convulse. Then he'd jogged toward her.

VIII

We'll go three months into the future now. Leave Rahil and Dr. Mudra's knowledge aside for just a bit. For you to understand that untruths, labels, and freedom all come together eventually, you must walk at my pace. I am not being condescending or intellectual. I too have grown to love the banality of the everyday, the security of a day job, and the landmarks on my commute to school. I've come to enjoy the smell of faint detergent on my bedsheets. We all must acclimatize to our world sooner or later, or else we'll end up wearing pants much larger than our frames.

I was stirring oats into cashew milk for Sara to consume; she had given up dairy for her arthritis. Rahil was out visiting his parents for the weekend. When you watch Sara eat, slowly, sweetly, wonderfully, you forget all you know about her. You also forget how much more you want to know about her. You can pause, splendidly, in the moment. You can watch her bring silver to her mouth, observe how her lips part as her eyes stay gently focused on the bowl.

We'd had our fights, we'd had our silences, in the past few months. And yet we were still here on her bed, only closer. Her Turkish music was on again. I didn't need her to lead me anymore; I now knew the influence Sara wanted to be on me. I dutifully closed my eyes and swayed my head left to right. I let my upper body move to the beat. Sometimes, if Sara let three or four songs play at a stretch, I could feel the beginnings of the ecstasy she described, the one she said our souls were connected to.

I heard the *clink* of the bowl on the nightstand, my eyes still closed, my body swaying. I felt her hands on my back, slowly, not suddenly, as if she had incrementally let her hand fall onto me. My eyes opened; we stared at each other. I kissed her, hard. I tasted her lips, her tongue, and even the nape of her neck. I felt a thousand lives kick at my gut, I felt something sacredly sad: the knowledge that this was the pinnacle of my joy, never to be experienced again.

It was not the first kiss or the last. I'd slept with Sara a month ago, and now it seemed to be the most ordinary of things to have done: I'd fallen in love with Sara and now she seemed to be the most ordinary of people to have fallen in love with.

After, when we were making tea in the kitchen, Sara quoted Kabir Das. My knowledge of Kabir Das, the fifteenth-century folk poet, was limited to my old Hindi textbooks. I zoned out of Sara's recitation, only for a second, to let this realization settle in: how pedantic my teachers had made the mystic seem.

> *Prem gali ati sankari, tamein dou na samai, Jab mein tha tab hari nahi, ab hari hai mein naahi.*

(Before I existed there was no God, and
now only he exists, not I, there is no place
for the both of us on this road.)

Sara knew how to twist my dormant insecurity; she
knew how to cut fresh wounds. These wounds were very
different from the ones I was familiar with: the death of
a husband, the death of expectations. No, Sara's wounds
weren't the ones that allowed you to regenerate or grow
scar tissue. Her wounds were the ones you take, like a
public lashing. The ones you let stay open, becoming a
part of you.

Not that she meant it personally. She'd say something
about universal love, about our collective consciousness,
about our bodies being rotten meat, and instantly my
purpose with her would be rendered insignificant. I had
spent so long trying to be of significance to her. Worked
so hard to be noticed in my individual capacity, my "true
friend" capacity. Always waiting to be acknowledged
as the person who grew with her. And it was in those
intimate times—making her food and feeding it to her,
stroking her hair and talking about her protected childhood or about college and Ketan—when she would say
something that obliterated me.

No, I was just a manifestation of our larger consciousness. A better, surer, muscular limb of consciousness, but just a limb nonetheless. Sara's mission was for
her body to accept the fact that her soul wanted out. She
demanded her body to let it go with dignity and peace.
I was just her body's soother, not a soul who could convince her to stay.

"We're on the same road," I told her, almost pleadingly.

She ducked her hand into the chamomile and pulled up a handful of the dried flowers.

"Yes, to the body's eye, we are two, three, even four, but to the soul it's just one. Mira, you depend so much on sentences of famous men and women, even my idea of Sufism required the validation of your Doris Lessing."

I stood there, taking in her confusing wisdom, which at first put me on the defensive. I had readied an argument to this. That the white man and the white woman were able to speak first because they'd had the platform, and now we too had privilege to speak of this Sufi wild love, when millions in our country didn't have the luxury of looking past their depleting incomes. Wasn't it then okay for privilege to use its privilege? And hadn't these arguments circled around my head for such a long time, when I'd read my grieving heart to bed? But here, to sick, sick Sara, I bowed my head. She was a true friend, seeing for me when I couldn't, for she understood something beyond words. Beyond good sentence construction, beyond Derrida and Camus and Aristotle. Beyond Rumi too.

She brought out a coaster and put it on the kitchen counter. Her spirituality could not erase the obsession with perfection. Her cups were lined neatly in the cabinet, the stove handsome and completely steel. Despite how much dust was floating around in this damn city, her house was as clinically clean as an American home in suburban California.

It was only then, in that moment, that I realized how methodically Sara's things were organized, dusted and pristine in their display. It was not the house that surprised me, but the fact that it had taken months for me to notice it was oddly immaculate. Had the need to be with Sara, to see her, to smell her, been that overwhelming?

She talked some more, standing over the counter. "Isn't it funny that the Koran, the Bible, and even the Gita tell us to pray? Because the more holy in prayer we are, the more the gods are pleased?"

She stroked the edges of the coaster and looked back at me. My face tilted, urging her to go on.

"Our translation of everything is wrong because we have not evolved yet. Yes, if we submit to God then we will be granted freedom, but submitting to God is not standing and praying, it is finding that God is everything, all of us. God is every bit of this moment, and when you realize this, you dance with relentless joy— that's the boon."

My intellectual barriers faltered when she said all this. She didn't sound like a new age self-help book. She sounded like an old soul who'd been sent back far too many times. A soul with a throat that had gone raw repeating the same simple thing.

You must be wondering about Rahil by now. But to understand—if not for you, then for me—I must go around and back, like a memory. At first Rahil didn't know that Sara and I had started sleeping together. Sleeping together so normally, so ordinarily. And when he did, he never confronted Sara. He got upset only with me. Rabidly upset, of course, because to share Sara's love is an impossible thing. To take the one individual who had explored her mind and make him secondary was one thing. But to take her body too—a wasting, rejected body, no less—the one physical manifestation of Sara's vast mind? It was too much.

Increasingly disorienting timelines help keep me from exposing the truth.

The truth was that I wanted to be in the right. I wanted to be simple. A good person acting primarily from a curiosity to live and to explore the boundaries of her existence. But no matter how many books we've read and how liberating philosophy can be, we are united in one wish. We're all scared of being the villain. We don't want to be that person—the one who exists selfishly for her own needs. We're scared to take individual responsibility for things unless our actions can be immediately glorified for their rebellious nature. I guess what I am saying is that I have written an unreasonably long preamble for something that is very simple.

Before I slept with Sara, I slept with Rahil.

IX

I wasn't even attracted to him, but I met him at a café called West of the City. It was the Tuesday following my canteen conversation with Dr. Mudra. I'd called in sick that day, didn't even go in for the first half as I'd originally planned.

The most powerful tool I had in my arsenal was the element of surprise. I had the knowledge—if only I could trust the authority of what my memory was telling me—that her seizure on the day we met was faked. And I was quite sure Rahil knew too.

By noon, my stomach started to cramp. I went to my bedroom, opened my laptop, and looked at old pictures of Ketan and me. Right after we got married, traipsing on Sri Lankan beaches. Drinking a Vietnamese iced coffee in Bandra on a brief trip to Mumbai. At home with Appa, who was wearing a lungi and a checkered shirt, smiling in the middle. What a different person I was. Cool, smart, but undeniably naive. The girl there was not me. In that moment I felt the thick possibility of an afterlife and shut the laptop quickly.

While I waited for the Uber, I thought about Ketan, living his afterlife, doing all the things he needed to do.

Was the life he had spent with me worthy of any new perspective? Or was his purpose in life to direct me to a new one?

In the car, I was overwhelmed with a simple kind of grief, one more becoming of a fresh widow. My body cried for Ketan, my heart ached for the simplicity of our time and the predictability of our love. Our dinners at home, our hand holding in bed. I was overcome with a desire to run out to the streets, drop to the ground, and beg the universe for it to return him to me. My eyes welled up, my heart spilled into the seat of the car, my mouth wanted to howl. Still, I knew from previous experience how it would play out. First I'd feel it coming like the tight twang of an impending migraine. And then it would hit. Whole moments of anguish would drown any sense of calm and pleasure I'd had minutes ago. But I knew my mind would protect itself from such grief, that if I just gave it a moment, I would regain composure. This was the first time in months, though. It used to come far more often, a couple of times a week. I dug my forefingers and middle fingers into my palms and waited for the mind to do its thing.

And it did. In moments, I was okay again. I looked at my phone.

I am here. See you in a few.

Be there in 10.

I put my phone back in my bag. Authoritative, strong, a true friend—I would be all of these things because I could. When my Uber pulled over, I walked out with confidence, strode right into the café, and found him: near the back, in a blue office shirt and khaki pants, cross-legged, and scrolling on his phone. He looked up at me with a big smile. His body was relaxed, open, and ready. My anxiety diminished before my butt hit the chair. He asked me if I wanted to order first, "to get it out of the way." We were on the same page. This café was nothing but an acceptable space for us to pour our hearts out about the woman who danced continuously in our heads. To the café we were far more banal, a married couple, two friends from work, anything but what we were. I ordered penne with mushroom and chicken, he asked for a basil pizza, and we both wanted iced lattes. We didn't mumble, we didn't make small talk. This was because I set the agenda with clarity.

"I need to tell you, before you start, I met Dr. Mudra, he talked to me after Sara left the hospital on Friday."

Rahil didn't bat an eyelid. In fact, he smiled again, pressed his back into the chair, and licked his bottom lip.

"Well, isn't that just serendipitous," he said. I looked him in the eyes, but only for a second, because he went right into it.

What Rahil Told Me About Sara

If there was one thing to pick up from the first half of what Rahil told me, it was an intense irritation toward Sara's parents. *Overprotective* was pure euphemism, and a term that Sara was forced to rely on. Rahil deconstructed the psychology of others clinically, with roaring emotional insights, making it impossible for me to believe he had anything to do with the corporate world.

When Sara was seven, her parents took her out of school and sent her to live with an aunt in Coorg. The children at Sara's school had been repeatedly stricken with bronchitis, and Sara's father was convinced it was the air quality. Her aunt mostly made fun of her parents over those months. "Crackpots," she'd call them. And Sara would lower her eyes and pretend she hadn't heard. Her aunt was a tall, overbearing lady who overfed Sara. At least that's what Sara claimed. Within a month her tummy bloated into a tight puff, and she tossed and turned at night, nauseated from all the food. When she complained about it, her aunt put a teaspoon of caraway seeds in her mouth. Her tongue blazed and her chest choked with its pungency. She stopped complaining.

Her parents retrieved her, of course, after the aunt made one too many passive-aggressive remarks on the phone. Once it became clear she didn't have time to look after her niece. This was just one of the stories Sara had told Rahil innocently, as if her parents had merely been idiosyncratically overconcerned. Like it was a passing fond memory from childhood, something that should only be laughed about together.

Then there were the stranger things that Rahil himself had to endure.

Sara's father meeting him in private, asking him too many questions about his plans, his health, his ability to provide. Sara's mother and father almost bending over backward to have Rahil at the house at all times. It wasn't because they especially liked him; they just knew the new truth. That Sara was in love with Rahil. They knew that Rahil had all the power; he could take their daughter away at any time. He could make her do dangerous things that could possibly kill her, hurt her, maim her. So they approached their village lion with caution and humility. They made the lion their guest.

Rahil stretched his arms out and looked down at his iced latte. "The thing is, I actually felt sorry for her mother, because, well, she knew."

One day, a year into their affair, Sara's mother had caught his hand when he was leaving to go back home. "Take her and go, she needs to see the world, Rahil."

Rahil shook his head in disappointment. "I took her out of the house, lived with her in another city, but I couldn't show her the world. The thing is, Mira, Sara already had too much of her parents in her by then. But I loved her. Even her mystical shit, I loved it all. I still do."

I didn't interrupt Rahil, didn't probe him or direct his answers. I wanted to let the afternoon drift into the evening, let sunset bleed into midnight. I wanted him to tell it his way, every little detail. And as Rahil spoke, my heart swelled with a new affection for him, one that hugged the aches of this man, one that appreciated the amount of thought and consideration he had taken to unravel Sara.

There was something missing from the moment they got married and moved into their new two-bedroom home in the new city. Sara was frightened when he left for work, and she was anxious until he returned in the evenings. She did not want to work; she didn't need to work. She obsessively read what Rahil referred to as pseudoscience blogs. But even in her utter passivity there seemed to be something potent within her. She was a being that had outside knowledge, the knowledge of human futility. Rahil admitted there were moments he believed in an intelligent awareness. If "God" was present, the evidence was Sara herself. Most of the time, though, he questioned if she was just depressed and self-centered.

For five months she successfully tutored four children in the apartment building in elementary social studies. That was the pinnacle of her happiness, because she had a rhythm to her day: four P.M., when the children would come, and six P.M., when Rahil would come home. She had to fill only the hours between nine and four. There had to be more to her banal domesticity. He'd felt it the moment he had met her.

One day he came early from work to surprise her with lunch from Thai Basil, but also because he'd grown worried about her. He could hear the music from outside the house, at least six notches higher than when she played it at home when he was around.

He opened the door and walked toward the bedroom, the music loud, daunting, throaty. She was lost in dance, her hair splayed in all directions, sweat glistening off her narrow, delicate face. A white T-shirt and a long blue denim skirt wrapped her intense thrusts. He watched her for minutes, but she didn't notice. He had to turn the music off for her to snap out of her trance. Only then did she look right up at him. The odd thing was her lack of embarrassment.

"There was my answer: she was more than just sick and depressed. I knew then, in order for Sara to be Sara,

I couldn't witness the moments that made her. Moments like this where I had no place."

She had invited him to dance with her, held him close, and whispered, "Feel the utter pointlessness of this world, submit to love, Rahil."

He didn't dance with her. He asked her if she needed anything, told her he had come just because he had a bad feeling. "I am fine," she said, smiling. And he left awkwardly back to work. In the evening the music was softer, sandalwood candles burning in the living room, and Sara stirring daal in the kitchen.

My pasta had arrived and so had his pizza. We picked at our food; we looked into each other's eyes, bravely, intimately. How could one person and his story tear down all my senses of social boundaries? All I knew was that I could look into this man's eyes silently. And he could meet my gaze without awkwardness. Our staring shared the mystery of a woman who centered our world.

"Rahil, what did Dr. Mudra say to you?"

I couldn't help myself now, I knew we couldn't sit here forever, and I didn't want to lose Rahil to something as silly as him having to go back to work. Rahil let out a playful "aaaaaah" from his mouth and ended it with a grin. A grin, I'll admit, that tickled my chest. "You know what Dr. Mudra and I have in common?"

"What?"

"We're both not psychiatrists." He chuckled into his remaining iced latte.

My face must have revealed only a violent impatience, because Rahil looked back at me and put his hands up in defense.

"Okay, okay, it's just that I've never said anything about Sara to others, but with you it's easy."

"So you think it's because of the way she was raised—all of her issues?"

Rahil picked up a crumb of pizza crust from his plate. He looked at the crumb as if it would answer my question.

An inexplicable rage was rising. I wanted Sara, but at the same time I wanted to shake her, I wanted to tell her she was stupid, annoying, fake, and a liar. And in that moment I wanted to shake Rahil too, for being so inconsistent with me. Flipping between talking about Sara's real issues and then flipping back to validating them. And then I wanted to shake myself, because none of these feelings made any sense. I looked at Rahil again, his lips still parted: sad, happy, intimate. I reached across the table and held his hand.

"How far is your place from here?" His voice cracked when he said it and my body lit up. I'd thought men who asked women to sleep with them so candidly existed only in the movies, American movies.

"Twenty-five minutes."

And I'd thought women who said yes with such confidence, at the spur of the moment, were only in the movies too.

X

My apartment felt different as soon as I entered it. Bringing in the potential for sex with a man can reimagine the architecture of your home. My old brown coffee table in the center of my living room was now a brand-new wooden table that Rahil saw before he had sex with me. My bedsheets, no longer old elephants on cotton, but plush white fabric where Rahil's naked buttocks rested. Where my face rested as he stroked me from the back of my head to the tips of my toes. My chipped red cups were no longer for coffee, but for the cold water we sipped after we had made love, had sex, fucked. And my rug in the kitchen wasn't just where I stood to cook anymore; it was the printed mat that Rahil stood naked on as he looked around for the chipped red cups.

The sex was needed, our bodies warmed and wanting, but the deed itself was perfunctory. We were searching for something else. Sex was the only way we knew how to look together for it. And we looked for hours. We withheld on intercourse for the longest time, knowing well it would last only minutes and signal an end to the longing, the hands in the hair, the pause in time. After cold water, we sat on my veranda in silence. My cell phone rang—it was Appa. I talked to him in front of Rahil, telling him I had just finished with school and had started teaching a history class. He started to talk about the Indian army's role in World War II, but I cut him off, promising to visit during the weekend.

Rahil had been staring intently at me as I talked on the phone. I wasn't sure if he was aware of it. That was the thing about Rahil—he seemed like a self-aware person. But did self-aware people blatantly stare? Or was it just his way of telling me he was interested in my life?

"Your father seems nice."

"He is."

Rahil shrugged his shoulders, stood up, and walked toward the living room. He started to gather his things off the coffee table: wallet, cell phone, coins. We didn't make any promises of secrecy; it was implied. We didn't make any talk of this being a one-time thing or even if it might be an every-chance-we-get thing. Our confusion but ready acceptance of the moment was implied.

Just as I thought he was about to say he was leaving, he sat back down on my sofa. He fiddled with his wallet, opening and shutting it. There was something endearing about him when he sat expressionless. It was only when he talked about Sara that his face looked focused and in control. I didn't know whether to sit with him or to encourage him to leave. Did he want to leave? Was he sitting around to make sure I didn't think it was only about a quick fuck? I walked closer to him, closing the veranda door behind me.

"Are you tired of taking care of a sick person?"

I wasn't quite sure what I thought I was going to get from asking this question. It wasn't because I wanted him to spill his frustrations with Sara. That would be too much of a betrayal—sleeping with her husband and then taking that opportunity to talk about her. If I remember correctly, my tone indicated that my question was not in fact a question. It was an offer. *Because I can switch out with you, Rahil. I can take your burden. I can take care of Sara.*

He looked at me and shook his head. "I think you should reframe that question, because you don't seem to understand that I love Sara very much."

"Right, that's why this is happening."

He raised his eyebrows at me. I felt unsure.

"I assume you care about Sara very much too. Do you?" Rahil asked with an unsettling amount of firmness.

I nodded.

He shrugged. "Right, Mira, so *that's* why this is happening."

I knew what it meant and I had no idea what it meant. The language of forbidden love has no common book. It's a series of coded sentences, its meaning created in the head of an individual and choked out to the other. Words that dangle between lovers, each of them finding the meaning they want to hear at that time. And what I wanted to hear at that time was that it was okay to love Sara. It was okay to love her and to find support and sexual intimacy with her husband at the same time.

When he left, I felt relief. I had needed him. But I also needed him to leave. Now, I could concentrate purely on Sara.

The following Friday was a government holiday, and school was off. Rahil was at work, and it was the first time I saw Sara after I had slept with him. I wasn't ashamed of what I had done with Rahil, so there was no guilt to show on my face. Sara talked only about her knees and about her parents wanting to come visit her. She then confided, "Rahil hates them, I know this. He thinks he plays it diplomatic with me, but I know." She chewed on a grape. Her fingernails were painted white and she wore a sky-blue linen kurta over white cropped pants. Even though I knew why Rahil hated her parents and even though I knew they were overprotective nuts, I felt an irrational anger rise in support of Sara. How dare Rahil hate her parents?

We made lunch together: daal with quinoa and cucumber salad. She was convinced quinoa would reboot her digestive system.

After lunch we listened to her music. Without a trace of hesitation I reached for her hair, stroked it, pulled her closer to me. She didn't resist, her musky rose bloomed into the air. Thick. Wanting. Hoping. It's not hard to make love to a woman, and it came easily to me. I had never really thought about a woman in bed before, but when I held Sara in my arms, hovered my hands over her nipples, and traced my index finger over her clitoris, I wondered why the idea hadn't consumed me before. Our kisses were often sloppy and always long. Different from the needy, thrusting tongue of a man. I could have kissed her for hours; I could have meditated sucking gently on her tongue.

"Isn't it all so outrageously silly, all of it?" she whispered into my ears. It was similar to what she had said to Rahil the day he found her dancing wildly at lunchtime. We dressed quickly when we realized Rahil would be home in an hour. When he came, we all went out for a stroll around the block, returning after twenty minutes when Sara complained of weakness. We ate dinner together, like three old friends, each one with a secret of their own.

A few times over those weeks, Rahil came to my house. Once when it was raining and he had been drenched from riding his two-wheeler, his thick hair plastered on his forehead, his eyes pleading. My heart ached for Ketan right then, and I found myself pulling Rahil in, taking his clothes off, and wrapping his body in two of the largest towels I had. He had pulled me close to him, naked underneath those towels. But I wanted him to wait. I needed to make him a cup of tea and calm the ache for Ketan in the minutes it took for the water to boil. By the time I got back to my sofa, Rahil's shoulders were covered by a towel and his boxers were back on. I set the cup down and Rahil put his arms out, offering me the warmth of his chest again. I rested my cheek on his stubble. I buried my nose into his neck. I hated how good it felt. How safe. How Ketan-like. He was the opposite of unstable Sara. Without him, Sara and I were waves of water crashing into each other. The tea stayed untouched as we made love on the couch. I imagined how good we must have looked: his body on mine, my left leg dangling off the sofa, my hair exploding onto the square Rajasthani print pillow. Like in the movies.

"What about Sara?" It was a question to myself, and I realized I'd said it out loud only when Rahil responded.

"She's fine with us, it's not like she won't sense it either."

I flung him off me. "What do you mean? She knows about us?"

"Sara's not that predictable, you know. I mean, I know she gets into her moments, but she might be more open-minded than you think."

I fixated on a hair on Rahil's leg, one strand caught in the spotlight of the sun. My eyes traveled to his eyes and I felt the rise of an unmistakable fear. Whatever trust that sex created between two individuals evaporated. Rahil's eyes had the ability to meet your stare back with an uncomfortable sharp focus. Like he had trained himself to stare back with confidence no matter what you said, what you questioned. At least in this moment he was. Whatever he was saying, he was manipulating me. I just couldn't say why.

"I would have killed my husband if he had slept with another woman."

Rahil laughed, his upper lip quivering. "It's obvious, you know? That you are attracted to Sara too."

I am not sure if he saw it, but I felt the panic shoot right into my eyes. I was quick, measured, my voice didn't crack. "I don't know what you are talking about. Sara is an amazing friend, and one that I don't ever want to hurt. But I understand that she is different and that you have—"

"Chill. Don't overexplain anything. You don't owe explanations to everyone. Be in the moment, Mira. That's something I've learned from Sara."

He started to nuzzle my neck again, his tongue whipping the side of my ear. I fell back; we tried to make love again, but lazily settled into each other's arms instead. I was secretly relieved, like I had won one over. *No sex again, Rahil, till I know what you're up to.*

"What does it feel like to keep trying to make Sara happy when she's so sick?"

He was quiet for a long time. He reached out for the tea that was stone cold. I reminded him it was undrinkable. He took the cup anyway and took a sip of the cold tea.

"It's nice to have someone who needs you all the time."

There. Now I've told you the truth, the meaty hiccups that had kept me from telling you my story straight. Every story is a matter of perspective, but to get perspective of any kind you must be able to tell your story with both subjectivity and objectivity. Your words must be thorough, ironed, inspected, and then catapulted into the arms of the world. Only then will the universe know what to do with you.

The fact that I had talked to Dr. Mudra weighed on me. The fact that he had not been clear with me about anything made me want to tell Sara in rebellion. The fact that Rahil and I found safety in each other? That made me want to run back home and pretend I hadn't walked into this new strange life. There were evenings when I sat between Sara and Rahil, tea and sweet whole grain biscuits spread in front of us. I imagined them hiding smirks in between conversations. I could swear I saw half-smiles directed at each other. Like they knew. They knew that I belonged to them, in different capacities. Most times it felt good enough, like I was cared for. That I had backup. Other days, I felt insecure in my own inabilities. I was able to get them to love me, but not enough to threaten their marriage. On rare days, I felt guilty about wanting to threaten their marriage.

It was a Sunday and Sara was drinking chamomile tea out of a white cup that I had never seen before. Rahil was out buying groceries and the quiet in the house made me restless. What makes a relationship enough? Why couldn't I just let things be as they were?

"I didn't tell you something."

I stuffed half a fennel-spiced biscuit in my mouth, wanting to take my sentence back. Sara's eyes looked right into mine. I covered my mouth with my hand as I chewed.

"Oh, about Rahil?"

Acknowledging anything about Rahil with Sara scared me more than what I wanted to tell her. Scared me more than what I wanted to provoke, but I could already feel the words push against my lips as they tumbled out.

"No, about your health."

She pursed her lips. "Oh, I thought you wanted to talk about Rahil."

She smiled, challenging me. Even if she did know about Rahil and me, why the hell was she smiling? I fought back.

"No, about your health. I talked to your doctor."

She sat up straight, alert. Her brown hair shook to the left. "Dr. Mudra? You talked to Dr. Mudra?"

Why did I enjoy her discomfort so much?

"Yes, I bumped into him at the hospital canteen. You had just left, and he mentioned that your health issues, you know, they might be more psychosomatic." That was a stretch of the truth, but it was the only thing that would provoke her enough.

"Are you calling me mentally ill? What did he say? So much for doctor-patient confidentiality. That old quack, I am going to report him."

"I am not saying you don't feel pain, but maybe it's caused because of stress, you know?"

Sara's face relaxed. "Is that all he said?"

"Yeah."

She half smiled. It's true Dr. Mudra hadn't told me what he really thought. But he'd made it quite clear that he did think something. I had never wanted to know so badly. I had never wanted to use her mystery as a weapon to hurt her. Until now.

"Maybe you imagine it, Sara."

What Sara Said to Me When I Told Her She Imagined It

She was silent. I started babbling from memory. About Foucault and mental illness. Trying to create a new bridge with Sara. Trying to find my way back to her. I talked some more, but her silence stayed. It hung eerily in the air. Abruptly, I stopped talking. She stood up and I saw that her eyes were bright with rage. I remember she was wearing sweatpants with a white kurta that ended at her small hips. She threw the first thing she laid her hands on, which, anticlimactically, happened to be a sofa pillow. It landed on my feet. I wanted to laugh, but I knew this was only the start.

She walked to the dining table and picked up an empty ceramic fruit bowl. She threw it at the wall and then rolled her head toward me and snapped, "I wanted to throw that fucking bowl at your head."

I had, perhaps, expected the throwing of breakable things, but not this verbalized intention. I was frightened for a shadow of a second that she might try to hurt me.

"After it all, Mira, after it all, all I try to tell you about life, about my fucking beliefs, my understanding of this stupid world, you go ahead and pigeonhole me as some rubbish mental case? Is that how fucking intelligent you are? With all your books and all your philosophers?"

Her dark skin was glowing. Her anger had allowed for beads of sweat to collect on the sides of her temples. I wanted to hold her, to take back everything I had said. I had said it to challenge her, because from the very day I met Sara there was a thumping need to call her out on something. Now that I had, it seemed futile, purposeless, and reckless. I held my hand out toward her.

"Sara, please, let's just talk this out."

She leaped toward her front door, swung it open and told me to get out. My fright came back, swiftly.

"And the stupidest thing, Mira, is you have no idea how ridiculous Dr. Mudra is, because you don't really know what he thinks. Hah, if you only knew that. But I don't care for snoops, I thought you were a friend, now get the fuck out of the house."

My fear protected me, and it told me to get out of her sight at once. I walked out of the house and took an auto-rickshaw back home.

As soon as I was home I texted her, *I love you*. She didn't respond. I texted Rahil, who told me to give her a few days, that she was really upset but it was nothing to worry about. I sat on my sofa with a fresh piece of paper and laid it on an old *Femina* magazine. I wrote her a letter. It felt weirdly good, but after twenty minutes my fingers and wrist were cramping—I couldn't remember the last time I'd written something this long with a pen. I listened to the hum of my building's power reserve; the city power had been out for the last two hours. It was at times like this I wished I had a cat around. Something warm and furry that allowed me to love it.

When I was done, I walked to my neighborhood post office for the first time. I stood in line for stamps. There were four booths open, three women in polyester saris and one potbellied man wearing a crisp white shirt. He was scratching his tummy even as he caught my eye. I asked lady number two how many stamps I needed for an in-city post. She didn't say anything back; she just took the letter, stamped it, and put it on top of a stack of envelopes. "It will reach tomorrow, ma," she said. Her accent was South Indian.

I can't remember anything more about that day, except for the fact that I cooked and ate rice, daal, chili fried mushroom, and mango pickle for dinner.

My Letter to Sara (For Michel Foucault)

Dear Sara,

No one writes letters anymore, and this might be the first and last one I write to you. Indulge me.

You know how much I read when I was at the farm that year. I know you don't have the patience or the inclination for the words of European men and intellectualism. But indulge me once more. Michel Foucault died in the '80s, and he is regarded, by those who like labels, as one of the most renegade existentialists and philosophers of our time. I'll spare you the intricacies of his life save for a couple of things. Less than a year before he passed away, he wrote a letter to his friend (and writer) Hervé Guibert. They were very close friends and the details of their intimacy are shrouded with a certain kind of mystery. Anyway, in this letter he wrote to Guibert, he details his obsession with watching a man who lived opposite to him. He watched him every morning at nine A.M. Here's an excerpt of the translated letter:

> **I have been wanting to tell you about the pleasure I take in watching, without moving from my table, a guy who leans out of a window on the rue d'Alleray at the same time every morning. At nine o'clock he opens his window; he wears a small blue towel or underpants, also blue; he leans his head on his arm, buries his face in his elbow; he does not move, apart from making occasional, rare, slow movements when he takes a puff of the cigarette he is holding in his other hand; but**

he is so tired that he is (almost) neither able to move the hand that holds the cigarette, nor to prop himself up; he gets tired moving along the railing of the balcony, his head rolling from one hand to the other; he then takes up his initial position, tucking his face back again in his elbow to look there for strong, intense, and powerful dreams, which leave him in a great (darn, [I need] more blue paper) depression; sometimes he makes a grand gesture with his arm that hangs freely or even his whole body; it is not that he is resting or trying to wake up; one can see that he is draping himself again in the night; and if he comes to the edge of his balcony it is not to cast light on the last shadows where he is caught, it is to show everyone, to no one (since it is only me who is watching him) that there is no day that can overthrow the gentle obstinacy that remains with him and sovereignly masters him.

The excerpt here ends with this line: "This morning the window is closed; instead I am writing to you."

If you were to take an academic approach to this letter, one might say this is post-intimacy, post-sexual, even post-friendship. This letter bears the soul of a simple, everyday obsession, with no call to action, no sentimentality, and no other fragments to build a story of friendship between Foucault and Guibert.

Sara, it is you whom I want to write like this for. I want to tell you about the lean wooden chair I sat on in the library at the farm. Its armrests folded out, so that I could prop my legs up; I always imagined it an effective chair to give birth to a child in. When I read those men and women, they gave me a strange comfort, an inkling that nothing was too dark, too out of place, too absurd. And when you feel that you can have a place in this world no matter how isolated you feel, then there is indeed a sense of liberation.

Anyway, I digress. It's time for me to come to the second part of Foucault, and that was his commentary on mental illness itself. Stay with me, Sara, because of this I am sure you will agree with him. He believed that the twentieth century brought science to mental illness. Right before that, the crazies, the sinners, the miscreants, and the dubious were put away and for all other practical purposes isolated.

But before isolation, there was a period of celebration, a society that appreciated the insane, thought of them as wise souls on a higher level of consciousness. Minds that expressed and responded to the world asymmetrically. And he believed all evil, or those men we chose to label evil, were simply an inevitable re-creation of our collective faltering. Evil people were simply mirrors of our everyday hypocrisies.

But then came the policing and the psychiatrists and the psychologists. All of them had not bothered with the "archaeology of knowledge" (as Michel Foucault put it)—going back into history and tracing our collective responses to mental illness itself. Our entire knowledge infrastructure of psychiatry has come from suppression and isolation. Where we pin down these people, suppress their tendencies, and coo them back into the "reality" we've semi-agreed to all agree upon. We can move on to the capitalistic society here and see how this baseline "reality" has been constructed, but it would be beside the point, and, really, I am already sensing your agitation and impatience as I write this.

Anyway, I am not sure what I want to communicate to you, but I'll try, and because there is no backspace in a letter, I'll let this be written out with no editing, no long pauses.

The thing is, Sara, I agree with you, that our "odd" responses to this world are coping mechanisms. And the oddest ones manifest in what we like to define and label. But your mind is special; it understands the absurdity of the world. It accepts it, and you allow yourself to reject the stupid everyday by willing yourself away from the world, by meditating on illness so that it can let your soul run away. I know this. But I also know that there is still this tired old reality we live in. It's one that you cannot deny. After all, you still need your chamomile tea and the love of Rahil and, hopefully, me. We are helpless and want you. Can't you at least consider reuniting your mind with your body and living with us in this moment? I am not special like you, Sara; my melancholy stemmed from having my ordinary expectations crushed, it was by chance that I could find relief in philosophy and the words of men and women who have died.

I want to be with you. Every day, trace your mind, your spirit. I want to write post-sexual notes to you. I want to live post-life with you. I am beginning to write words that make no sense. So I'll stop here. Because if anything, I want you to make sense out of me.

Yours,
Mira

XI

I visited Appa with an agenda. It was the type of agenda that comes quickly, makes you think, Why hadn't I ever had the courage to do this before? The more valuable question was this: Why hadn't I been compelled to demand the answer to this question?

Of course I had the answer to that one nestled in my head. I now had time. And while I had to play it cool with Sara and Rahil, I still felt the excitement of being a part of them. I felt a sinister void threatening to infiltrate my body and numb my mind. It terrified me and made me think of my mother. At school, at lunch, and right before my eyes felt heavy at night. My mother haunted me. My mother who had chosen to be sad instead of loving me. I could see her point of view now. Love was not an easy thing to dole out in exchange for the ordinariness offered to her by life. An ordinary daughter or an extraordinary melancholy? At least a piercing sadness could make her feel. Just like how Sara made me feel. Sara, anything but ordinary.

Before this, I hadn't thought about my mother very much. When she'd died, there was no real grief. People expected me to cry and feel lost, and I played the part as best as I could. I suspected my father had done the same too. But I was just sixteen. She'd had a gallbladder infection that spread to her blood. Or at least that's what I was told. When aunts and uncles from other parts of the country huddled around us just after she passed, there was the shock of her immature death, but there was also a wall of eerie silence. Some people in that house knew things I didn't.

Appa sat on his couch. He was irritated with me—my weekly visits had become biweekly, and he was convinced there was a man in my life. "When I've supported you through everything, been as liberal as I have, why would you hide this from me?"

"There is no new man, Appa!"

He shrugged his shoulders in defeat. I reached for a milk biscuit that he'd laid out on the table, just as he put his hands together and pushed them out into a stretch. He looked into my eyes briefly. I felt an earnest guilt creep from my gut. He was always there for me, always on my side. But he wasn't built to support or even counsel on the things I was doing. My situation was too far past my own worldview; I couldn't imagine how Appa would begin to react. That kind of truth might destroy something fundamental in our relationship.

There were other truths that I was beginning to believe we could handle sharing. I chewed on my lip and considered letting the anxiety of the question get the better of me. It didn't. This time would not come again soon. I looked straight at Appa.

"Appa, I want to talk about Ma."

Appa grinned. "Well, she would be proud of you: teaching children, giving back to this country..."

"No, Appa, you and I both know that Ma barely managed to keep up with life itself."

"Mira, she loved us very much, what is this about?"

"You know what it's about."

He cleared his throat. I closed the World War II book that lay open on the coffee table. I could not have anything else distracting him, nothing that could derail him from answering my questions. I felt stupid as soon as I did it, though, so I flipped it back open and looked at him expectedly.

"Did she really have a gallbladder infection?"

"Of course she did, you were there at the hospital—what kind of question is that?"

It's true, I did remember my mother in pain one night, going to the hospital, being admitted into a private room with a small TV that I fiddled with. I remembered the movie *Maine Pyar Kiya* was playing, with Salman Khan wearing a hat labeled "friend". I remembered the heroine, Bhagyashree, in her bright yellow sari romancing Salman Khan by the lake. The tune of the lake song started to whirl in my head. I remembered the doctor, bearded, murmuring to my father. But after that it was all a blur, and forty-eight hours later she was dead. I had to leave school early; my father's sister picked me up. She was dead on the bed, her face relaxed, peaceful, almost happy looking. I remembered not knowing what to feel, too guilty to ever admit the word that came to me hours later: *relief*.

"Appa, what was wrong with Ma? I mean, do you

know why she was depressed? You realize we've never actually talked about this. After everything that happened with Ketan and me."

I was well aware it was a question that sounded like it had been asked by a fourteen-year-old. Some questions come too late.

Appa let out a sigh, then he stood up. I panicked—for a second I thought he would burst into tears. Instead he came to my side of the sofa and sat by me. He put his arm over my shoulders, then his forehead to mine.

"No one is like everybody else; everybody has their own purpose, Mir-Mir."

I shook Appa off. I demanded more with my eyes.

What Appa Told Me About Amma

Appa met my mother through a family friend. Their marriage was arranged and both parties were neither desperate to get married nor opposed to the idea. My father had a good job, my mother had finished college but had never worked. He thought she was pretty, sweet, and mysterious. They had six dates before they got married. She talked a lot at that time. She was an excited girl, wanting to set up house, host dinner parties, have babies.

If she were the same woman today, she would have been a feminist advocating and supporting women who wanted to housekeep full-time. She loved the idea of it, even though her own mother had taught college-level economics her entire life and her parents had offered her opportunities and money to study further. Appa would create history quizzes for her, and she would indulge him. They'd talk on the phone for hours, about movies, history, and Appa's job. She wanted to experiment with new recipes, decorate the new house. All she could talk about was becoming the perfect wife. In fact, Appa, who would have supported and encouraged a working wife, felt like it would be too cruel to even suggest it to my mother. If this was her happiness, then it would be his too, and his conservative parents would be just as happy.

I didn't interrupt Appa when he told me these parts. I wanted to—I wanted to stop him and say, *Are you sure? Is this really true?* Because despite having heard about this version of my mother, I couldn't for a second picture my mother as a happy woman, a woman enthralled by keeping house and wanting to have a child. The mother I remembered lived in her head, listless, meandering, wandering the house like a ghost.

They got married and a few hundred relatives came—a moderate-sized wedding. Appa had never wanted to live in the same house as his parents, and it created a stir. But they found a house close by and the dramatics ended.

Ma had the house painted bright colors: yellows, oranges, and greens. She spent weekends making lists of carpentry work to be done, drew up blueprints for quaint little cupboards in the kitchen and bookshelves in all the rooms. The house was filled with laborers for a month as they hammered, chiseled, made the home my mother had in her head.

Every morning she dutifully walked to Appa's

parents' house. She offered them prasad from the morning puja, complained about rising vegetable prices with her mother-in-law, and read the small print in the newspaper for his father. She never really bothered to see her own parents much, apart from Diwali and special occasions; they had an older son and they were well taken care of. "I was a reluctant patriarch, Mira, she did it all on her own accord. Sometimes I thought it was silly, this bright convent-educated woman, so intelligent, acting like some TV-serial bahu."

I sensed this response was more for me than my mother. Appa always wanted me to regard him as more liberal than he was. He was too well read to position himself any other way. But I knew my father well enough to know that he'd probably enjoyed these qualities of this unknown mother of mine.

Every evening, my mother would have dinner ready at eight. My father would come home in the early evening, and they would chat about the day, she would excitedly tell him about a new recipe she wanted to try, or her fight with the grocery store guy, or a new friendship she had made with someone in the neighborhood.

A year later she was pregnant with me. The first months were glorious; she had no nausea and an unusual energy. Her face was lit up, pink, and she wore bright, festive saris. She made a lot of sweets the first six months of her pregnancy—ghee-laden laddoos, milk sweets, toasted rava with nuts, and gulab jamun—all from scratch. She and Appa went on a week's vacation to Coonoor, where they stayed at a guesthouse overlooking dense tea estates. They took long early-morning walks, drank chai from kerosene stoves, sipped tomato soup at night, and giggled under the blankets. It was the best vacation they ever had, and they were excited for their first child.

The pregnancy became harder at seven months; she had cramps and her energy shot down. But it didn't stop her from smiling or cooking. Her mother-in-law made sure she ate meals prepared in accord with family tradition, insisting on ghee and milk to ensure the child was fair. My mother laughed about it, but my father was angered and he had a huge fight with his mother about her fairness obsession. Appa spent too much time telling me about this fight, leading me to wonder if it was just a white lie. The more details he went into, the more it seemed like a desperate cry for validation. I wanted to tell Appa that his younger self didn't have to match the progressive mind of the present, but instead I just nodded my head, wanting him to go on.

I was born in a small birthing center. A friendly nurse told Appa to come and see me forty-five minutes after my mother had a very smooth and normal delivery. She was exhausted but ecstatic. Everyone was there, both my sets of grandparents. The nurse took a picture of all of us right there in the room.

My mother sang to me, cooed to me, dressed me up, and massaged my limbs with coconut and sesame oil. She'd sit and watch Hindi films from the '80s, pointing at heroines and heroes and telling me about them as I wiggled in her arms.

"She talked to you like you were an adult even at six months. She explained movie plots, she was obsessed with Anil Kapoor."

And then my father told me something I had never heard before: he came home from work one day when I was seven months old, and the home was unusually quiet. He found my mother sitting in the living room staring into space. "Where is Mira?" he asked. She didn't reply. He went to her and yelled. That's when she looked up and said with leveled calmness, "I am not sure."

I was in the bedroom, of course, but I had been un-attended to since four o'clock, when our maid, Radha, had left to attend a wedding. My mother had not fed me, nor had she touched me the entire day. Or at least that's what Radha claimed when she returned the next day. It took a month or so of my mother's erratic behavior for my father to realize she needed a doctor. She was diag-nosed with postpartum and told to eat healthy and exer-cise. But she never recovered and slowly whittled into a world of her own—one where new recipes, bookshelves, and shopping for baby clothes did not exist. My mother quite literally changed who she was seven months after I was born.

She switched on and off when it came to simple tasks, and my father was in denial, he now admitted.

"I trusted your amma would return to her regular self. I would have to just wait it out for a year, that's what the doctors had predicted."

My father relied on his mother and Radha to bring me up for the first couple of years. Soon enough, though, he accepted the new mother. The bright, happy house-wife was a distant memory, like a character he once knew from a book he had read as a child.

"And, Appa, her death?"

This time Appa did not pause. He looked at me, his face relaxed, calm. He had finally accepted I wasn't here to hear old stories. I was here for the truth.

"She did have an infection, Mira, and it was serious."

I sat very still. I could hear my breath.

"But she also had a bottle of sleeping pills with her, in her hospital room. She took more than twenty of them, and by the time we realized something was wrong, her medical complications just did her in. She was willing her body to go anyway; she just gave it a kick start."

My body began to shake involuntarily and deep, hiccupping sobs rose from my throat. I felt release, I felt okay. I was crying because it felt good, it felt good that Appa could tell me something I had always sensed. I hugged Appa and held him for longer than I ever had. He patted my back; his feet on the ground were tapping to some unknown rhythm in his head.

XII

A few weeks after my conversation with Appa, I'd been restored to my place in Rahil and Sara's lives. The process had been slow. One night Rahil called me. I was thrilled because I hadn't texted him first, he had sought me out.

His voice was tender. I imagined him looking over his shoulder to see if Sara was near. But that couldn't be true because he said he was at work. He told me to watch this one documentary on Netflix. I was intrigued. Not with the documentary, but the fact that Rahil was interested in true crime. When I asked him about it he told me he went through a serial killer phase. "Ever hear of Jeffrey Dahmer?"

He went into detail about him and I couldn't help but giggle. Rahil was such a straitlaced guy, tame, almost shy. I wondered if he was just googling in real time and pretending to have some sort of fascination to make himself more interesting. To court me. I felt that thrill rise again. I asked if I could come see them soon.

"Soon," he said.

Rahil told me he had read my letter too. It didn't bother me. By this time I had already made peace with the fact that both Sara and Rahil knew the extent of our relationship. Why did we keep our most obvious secrets away from each other? Because this is how we thrived, how we bloomed. Once you start talking about things, jealousy emerges and everything becomes a mess.

Sara found my letter hilarious. It was "begging for intellectual validation." That's what Rahil said. "But she thought it's funny that you think she is insane and she told me she's just going to ignore that part about you."

An hour later, my phone had buzzed with a text. All of a sudden, there it was again, this persistent odd question.

Has Sara showed you any medical tests in the last weeks? Just wondering, cuz she tends to hide them from me.

He was lying. Sara didn't hide anything from him. She couldn't. I remembered her stack of files neatly organized and tucked in between the old magazines near the dining table. Besides, why would Sara show me something on her medical records that she wouldn't want Rahil to see?

No. And why? This is the fourth or fifth time you've asked. Do you feel like she is hiding something from us?

No. Never mind.

I felt a whirl of nausea in the middle of my stomach. It passed. I set my phone down and looked at the fan. It tended to *clickety-clack* instead of *whirr*.

A week later, I was pulled back into their company, their dinners, their blue teacups. Rahil and I still met for coffee sometimes, but we hadn't slept together since the fight with Sara. When we talked now, it was as close friends who tided each other over the confusion of what we were, what we meant to each other. He listened to me. He talked back, asked questions. Sometimes I talked about Appa, other times I talked about the books I read and the onus I carried of finding meaning in the mundane. He didn't dismiss like Sara; with him, there was nothing to prove. He was present. He was gently assertive. But his words and body failed to explicitly hint at the possibility of sex. Not that I had asked. I knew it was an unsaid game with unsaid rules. Something about that fight had allowed Sara to be in power. Almost as if Rahil was a caretaker, a watchman, a guide to the relationship between Sara and I. But one thing was clear: Rahil's primary responsibility and priority was Sara. It was in the way he looked at me when I sat by him. Always making sure to keep a comfortable distance. It was in the way he called Sara for dinner as I followed her to the table. It was in the way he took over the kitchen, spending long periods crafting her meals.

On a Tuesday I was sitting with Sara on the couch. She had started eating normally a couple of weeks ago, but in the last three days she'd begun complaining of mouth ulcers.

"Let me see."

"No, they are ugly."

I put my fingers to her lips, she flinched and swatted at my hand.

"You don't understand, it's not like I am not hungry, but I have to keep myself from eating, it's destroying my body."

I could have taken the commonsense route and given her the basic rationale behind nutrition, but you can't play such a primitive card with Sara.

"Is there something we can make that you think your body will, I don't know, like, thrive on?"

She tilted her head in exasperation. "I can't stand Rahil pestering me on and on about food, it's like I am ten again, it's so annoying. I am not starving myself, I am eating. I just don't like him serving me all the time. I can't tell him that either—it's like I've told him I want a divorce or something. I mean, that's how sad he looks."

If there was one thing I could swear my truth upon, it was how much Sara depended on Rahil's coddling: how her body sighed in relief with every look of concern, every hug, and every cheek stroke he offered her. Maybe I helped. Sara needed the same amount of concern from me. I could only hope.

"Well, if you are stressed about that, I mean, that's probably causing your ulcers in the first place." I could hear Rahil in the kitchen. "Want me to tell him not to bring you any food now?"

"No, it's okay, just go help him. You're right, I'm making this a bigger deal than it should be."

I walked into the kitchen. Rahil was fiddling with her bowl of oats. He jumped like a cat when he saw me, and the spoon clattered to the floor.

"What?" he demanded coldly, startled. Ketan would have never talked to me that way.

I looked at the bowl. "What are you doing?"

"Don't come in here when I am cooking, it makes me very uncomfortable."

I wanted to tell him that preparing oats hardly counted as cooking. I wanted to tell him that Sara would not eat anything he made. I wanted to ask him what he was doing standing over her bowl, fiddling with what? Sometimes I overthought things, it's true. But most of the time I felt like this house had too many secrets. Maybe I didn't want to know those secrets. But I found strange pleasure in telling myself that they existed.

My doctor at the farm had told me I overthink to the point of creating delusions, and that overthinking is a process of self-destruction. I agree with this in theory, but with Sara and Rahil it was different. Sometimes overthinking is as utilitarian as a seasoned chess player studying her board for thick minutes before she makes her next move. What if my doctor was right? My toes curled involuntarily. Chipped blue polish. What parts of this relationship were just in my head?

"It's oatmeal, for God's sake." I waved at the bowl to make my point. He slapped the bowl with his palm; it rocked and moved two inches farther away. What the ever-loving fuck was he trying to do? Was I suspicious now? Yes. Was I possibly more upset by the fact that he hadn't bothered asking me if I wanted a bowl too? Maybe. Why was it only Sara who needed the spoon-feeding? Why was I the one who gave off that I-don't-need-to-be-coddled vibe?

"Actually, I don't think Sara is hungry. We were just chatting and she said her mouth is really hurting." I pushed myself toward the kitchen table and nudged the bowl toward me. "But I wouldn't mind some."

"What's with you, Mira? It doesn't matter if she isn't hungry, she has to eat small meals every few hours, you know that."

"No, you know that." I felt thoroughly stupid as soon as I said the words. In a panic, I grabbed the bowl. There wasn't a spoon in sight; I dipped my finger into it. My lumpy-oatmeal-covered forefinger rose as a sign of victory. I put it in my mouth and sucked. "It's masala flavored, that's disgusting. I thought Sara prefers fruit in hers," I said with a stoic confidence.

Rahil had frozen all this while, staring at me like I was a new person. A drama queen of sorts he had never calculated for. He slapped the bowl out of my hand. The plastic bowl bounced twice and splattered the turmeric-stained oatmeal all over the floor.

His voice dropped to a firm whisper: "Why don't you trust me? Do you know that Sara is doing this to torture me? She did have an ulcer on her bottom lip, but she won't let it heal, she fucking chews on it till it bleeds. She bites her lips at night until they're freaking raw. So yes, now she can't eat because it hurts too much to put anything into her mouth. And you know why? Because of all this. All of this stress. She can't figure out how she feels about you...about us... the three of us."

My eyes immediately started to water. I was the problem. And now I was responsible for Sara's raw bleeding lower lip. I choked out a whisper: "Maybe she's protecting herself from you, maybe your coddling reminds her of the way her parents were. She's not a possession."

I started to clean up, wiping the oatmeal away and discarding the plastic bowl in the sink. My heart was thumping with sorrow. Did I have to protect Sara? I couldn't trust myself anymore. Rahil had resigned himself to the corner of the kitchen, his face defeated and pulled. Irrationally I felt sorry for him. Maybe it was hard, finding his unique way to love Sara when there was another person willing to compete for her. Maybe my time with Sara on the bed swaying to Sufi music seemed competitive to Rahil. Maybe the way I made her tea annoyed him. Maybe he just needed his own way to love Sara.

I put my hand on Rahil's shoulder. "Don't treat me like a stranger, you know how I feel about you."

My body winced in preparation for rejection, but he surprised me and pulled me toward him. I inhaled. Wood, sweat, Rahil. My body flooded with reassurance, safety. For a moment, I could smell Ketan. My heart slowed.

"I am figuring this out too, you know, Mira, but you have to respect that Sara is special. We both need to help her."

I squinted. "Yeah."

"Let's not talk about it now." He offered another hug. I pushed out of it in seconds. He looked at me, confused.

"Why don't you make her another batch of oatmeal." The authority and confidence in my voice faltered. "I'll go check on her."

"Let me check on her first," Rahil said right back.

The balance of power in the house was almost in harmony. Sometimes it was like Rahil and I were Sara's parents, but I didn't like to think about it that way, it was too weird. Everything was weird enough as it was.

As soon as Rahil left the kitchen, I went back to the abandoned bowl in the sink. My heart started to pound again. Maybe he really had gotten that upset because I'd interrupted one of the few things he was left to do for Sara since my arrival. But the jumpy startle I'd given him by simply walking into the kitchen? It didn't add up. I picked up the bowl and looked at the remnants of goopy oatmeal left clinging to the sides of the blue plastic. I sniffed at it. It smelled like mustard-tempered oatmeal, with a hint of something sweet that I couldn't quite identify. A dark idea started to form. The idea became more pronounced in seconds.

I stopped my head from filtering in any more questions; it was ungrateful of me to think like this about a man who had given me so much solace. A man who had offered me comfort and love. Sara was no fool; she would have noticed if her very own Rahil was the cause of her problems. Surely. I glided my finger along the side of the bowl and raised the oatmeal to my lips. I let it sit on my tongue. It didn't taste weird. It was really very good. I bit my lip in guilt. The quick sting on my lower lip made me feel better. A physical punishment for over-thinking.

I set the bowl down and started to make some more oats. I added enough to the water for two servings. That's when I heard Sara humming as she entered the kitchen.

"All good now, Rahil gave me some numbing gel for my mouth. He told me he spilled a bowl of masala oatmeal, so I am thinking, would it be too much to ask you for a banana and brown sugar version instead?" She winked and I laughed. I knew Sara preferred her oatmeal sweet. And here she was, magically ready to eat. "Rahil just thinks his masala oats are the best, plus it gives him another chance to add a bunch of turmeric to it, you know, anti-inflammatory..."

"Where's Rahil?" I asked, mostly to know if it was okay to make fun of his masala oats recipe.

She waved her hand. "Taking a shower now."

Together we made bowls of sweet oatmeal. Sara chopped two bananas into perfect circles and arranged them on top of each bowl. I sprinkled the brown sugar on top. Sara curled her lips in thought. "Hmm, maybe a dollop of coconut oil?"

"That's the most hipster meal I've seen in a while," I said, and with that sentence the relief of normalcy buzzed through my head.

Later, Rahil sat across from us as he read a book. He watched us on the couch for the next hour, sitting like two old friends who had been reunited after years. Giggles and brown-sugared bananas. There was no talk of illness, there was no tension. Could it be this easy?

I decided to go home for the night. I didn't have any worthy clothes to wear for school the next day and, oddly, even though I'd had so much fun with Sara, I wanted to sleep in my own bed. A private space to soak in the day. A place that I knew bowed to my power. Pillows and bedsheets meant only for me. Plus, I didn't want to be a burden to Sara. I wanted Rahil to be the reason for her ulcers and night chewing, not me. I couldn't afford that.

I took off my jeans and rubbed the red welts right below my belly button. I tried to remember if this pair had always been tight or if I had gained weight. I couldn't remember. For whole minutes I was just Mira again. I didn't think about Sara and Rahil, my nighttime ablutions insulating me from them. I picked up my red toothbrush, measured out a dollop of Ayurvedic toothpaste on the bristles, and started to brush. I had taken to nighttime brushing only because I was having sex. The last time I had been so particular about my oral hygiene was when Ketan was around. He would make sure I brushed before we went to sleep.

I sat in bed with a wad of cotton and nail polish remover. Studiously, I wiped out all traces of dark nude from each finger. It hadn't even chipped or anything, but it didn't matter. I admired my naked nails for a minute and took a sniff of the bottle; the acidic twang reminded me of being thirteen. My mother wiped off my nails every Sunday because they checked at school. She did so robotically, but I enjoyed the vigorous rubbing: it was contact; my mother had to hold my hand to do it. Now that I thought about it, I was sure I'd put on nail polish every Friday afternoon just so my mother could rub it off on Sunday evenings.

I ran the fan on the highest speed and settled in. Only then did I allow Sara to pop back in my head.

Rahil filtered through every few seconds but I pushed him away. Sara gave me the quiet thrill that I needed.

That night I dreamed of Rahil. I was in the kitchen again, but it wasn't in their house or mine. It was that magic trick the mind plays after dreaming, when you just know where you were but you can't remember what it looked like. Rahil was offering me a bowl of oatmeal. It had ripe, bursting red strawberries on top. I held out my hands for the bowl. "Wait," he said with an almost mischievous grin. From his left hand he sprinkled something on top. I thought it was sugar.

He came closer to me—I could feel his breath. "Do you want some?" he asked seductively.

"Yes," I said. I wanted it. I could taste the sweet tang of the strawberries.

He put the bowl in my hands. I looked down at it. A hundred dying moths wallowed inside, their wings caught in lumps of oatmeal.

XIII

Days washed in like the ocean thinning onto sand, then retracting into the thick mystery of its depth. Ebb and flow. I remember moments from that time, mostly not in order. I remember standing outside Chai Wallah, the fancy tea shop that served sweet chai in cups made from clay. One hand held chai, the other scrolled texts from Appa and Samina. Appa's were forwarded news article, ones I wouldn't ever read. Samina sent an update about a freak lynching in a small northern town.

Rasaguras are getting people killed.

The culture police of the country wanted people to respect that Rasaguras came from only one place because it was divine. Now people were buying the fruit in bulk and eating it like it was a common banana. *It's a fruit that should be eaten like one would eat prasad from a temple,* raged one minister. Seven men from a town I had never heard of before decided another man was disrespecting the fruit and lynched him. I remember not caring, even though I received the same story Samina was referring to in one of Appa's forwards. Even though I knew I could analyze the politics endlessly with either of them. And last year I probably would have.

The street in front of me blared horns, but the rain had settled the dust. A beige stray licked its paw, its tail curled for warmth in the unexpected coolness. I stood on a broken rock lying in the middle of the sidewalk and looked through Samina's text again.

Mrs. Mira, perhaps it's a larger class conflict here, and the fruit is just the scapegoat?

There was something about Samina. Something tragic, something that made my heart twist. She was looking to dump her mind into the world without understanding how very complex it was. I found myself swell with an unfamiliar irritation. I could not admit it to myself back then, but I was envious of young Samina possessing an intellectual curiosity I once had—one that had sustained me. I remember not replying to her text.

I remember shopping on Gandhi Street. In retrospect it was odd I was taking time to do something as mundane as shopping. Perhaps it was the idea of bangles and how Sara might like them on my wrists. Or maybe it was the one fantasy I had of Rahil stroking my face and the red glass bangles clinking gentle jingles as I moved my arms to his face. There were small vendors laced back-to-back in between wooden carts of boiled corn rubbed with chili powder and men offering stale samosas and fresh chaats from rickety wooden trolleys. I had picked the peanut guy. His face was alive; his eyes blinked to the rhythm of the metal spoon hitting the giant tava. Inside the giant black utensil were peanuts—roasted, smoky, earthy. *Tang-tang-tang,* he'd hit the side of the tava every few seconds in a bid to get public attention. His hair was cut short, his fingernails dirty, and his teeth bright white.

"For you, madam, special, I even have onions and chili powder to mix with them, come have some now and you won't even realize your boyfriend is late to meet you."

I had to laugh. "Only a small bit of chili powder and extra onions."

"And a bit of lime juice," he said, and grinned. I watched his fingernails press against an already-squeezed lime and imagined Sara cringing at the thought, especially raw produce grown God knows where and laid out to the sun and smog. I wondered if it was just envy that compelled such judgments. The fact that her body couldn't eat the delights of the streets. Or maybe this was why I was here, to do the things I didn't do with Sara.

I don't remember much else about my time alone in this period.

All that is certain is that I still needed the restless love of Sara. Perhaps it was the same thing Rahil had with her too. I had held Sara naked in my arms many times. Each time I held her, I felt silly about the pedestrian safety that was my love for Rahil. Each time I made love to her, I imagined the greatness of life, the things I could be, the things I could do. I felt important, wise, and significant to the universe. It was baffling that most of the time I was kissing her body, I was thinking of all the incredible things I had read and wanted to share with her. When I grazed my hands over her nipples, I felt the future. I fantasized: *I am a professor of philosophy in a European country, maybe Germany, maybe Brussels. I am an important writer, touring the country, Sara with me. She's sitting in the audience, her face covered in pride. I am living with Sara in a small hill town, we run a café where famous writers come to*

*write, away from the city. They sit around over espresso, and
Sara and I impress them with our ability to converse on any
subject.*

It was only after we made love that I thought of Rahil. Of his role in Sara's life. Of his role in our life. And
the fantasies started to lose their importance. I'd feel
my tongue ready for the wet warmth of chamomile tea.
Rarely would I want to cuddle and lounge around in
bed after making love with Sara. The ecstasy faded into
something reliable: casual banter, Rahil's dinner menu,
the need for the TV to be on.

Sara's health had been stable over the last month.
While nothing had dramatically spiked, her fatigue,
headaches, and cramps remained. Rahil and I never discussed the oatmeal incident and that nightmare faded
into obscurity. He now allowed me to make tea for Sara,
and I allowed him to fiddle in the kitchen alone when
he wanted to. The ordinariness of our everyday interactions had made me feel only guilt for housing dark
thoughts about Rahil.

Our new routine was addictive. It was the drug I
woke up to and sustained with undivided commitment.
I gave up chatting with the schoolteachers after school
so that nothing could swing the clockwork of happiness we'd built. I had semi-abandoned my house by
this time, coming straight to Sara's house at four, when
we made love. Then we had tea ready for Rahil by six. I
can't imagine he didn't smell our sex in the room, filtering through peppermint. It cut through the perfume of
chamomile, it radiated from Sara's cheeks, and, most of
all, it sweated itself out from the pits of my arms.

I told Sara about my mother, weeks after my conversation with Appa. When I spent time with Sara, it was like my past had no consequence. I felt intrusive when I talked about myself. So I waited it out, knowing that my stories would find a way for Sara to hear them. And when she did, Sara nodded her head vehemently, stroking my face with a beige-painted nail. "Her soul was dying to get out, so sometimes a baby lets your mind wind down. It allows your soul to be set free. You can't possibly blame yourself—you were what she needed."

I could have turned it into a fight very easily; I could have slapped her then and there. I had never seen a happy mother, and I was the reason for it. All this pro-death nonsense Sara spouted, it enraged me, but it also drew me to her. At that moment, I chose to be drawn to her instead of angered. I wept. She whispered into my ears—I can't remember what, but it helped.

We were sitting on her sofa; she turned back to her computer. She showed me a new article on seizure treatment, a new medication, a trial testing in the United States. My throat tightened; she had not spoken of her seizures in a long while. She still had crippling joint pain and headaches, but she had not found the need to have another seizure. I believed now, after watching her these many months, that she tricked her body into creating them on demand. She willed them, and with as much ease she willed them away. It was the fatal flaw of psychiatry, I surmised, to not evaluate the true potency of the mind over the body.

She could die at any moment, I suddenly thought. It made my entire body flinch in panic. I pushed the idea away, temporarily soothed by the calmness of her voice. Nothing could take away such calmness before its time, no universal force could reckon with it. And the thought would diminish for a while, only to rise again, usually in the middle of the day, when I was correcting papers.

One weekend she casually told Rahil and me that she'd had a seizure the past Thursday afternoon. We were heaped with guilt. Automatically our shoulders sagged, we muttered apologies. We were not with her full-time, but the mere suggestion of Rahil working from home made her hysterical. Sara needed her hours alone—of this I was sure. She was in no mood for apologies.

"I am alive, don't worry." Then she shocked us by saying she wanted to go out for a walk. Alone. Rahil signaled with his hand from behind her to let her go. I nodded my head, but asked if she wanted company to the gate.

"You stay with Rahil, our dinner plan is still the same."

I awkwardly sat back down. Sara waltzed out of the house with the confidence only a body that had never felt an ache could. Rahil rubbed his left eye as if he were buying time to make sure Sara was really out of the house. Finally he looked at me, his face soft and endearing.

"She's upset. I mean, upset about us. I mean, she wants more control in it. She likes the idea of it all. You know, the three of us, but she's been insecure lately, that's why..."

My gut was tangled. This was as open as we'd ever been about the three of us since the oatmeal fight. "Rahil, I don't know how to talk about this, but I just want everything to be like this, forever, without upsetting anyone."

He exhaled and sighed. My foolish want had obvious answers.

"And I want world peace too while we're at it," I said, trying to make light. He didn't respond. Anger flooded. "I am taken for granted here. You know, sometimes I think you like her being this way, so you can feel important."

He rose, went to the side bar, flipped a glass, and poured a large measure of whisky. He pushed the glass toward me. I swallowed in utter exhaustion. Rahil didn't fight back with words.

He took his left thumb and stroked my cheek. "I'll always love you, Mira, but you have to understand, there are things you can't... you know... can't understand."

"There's nothing wrong with her. Look at her, she had a seizure, but she's out there taking a walk now. Maybe you need to stop coddling her so much, enabling her so much."

"Tell me you've not kissed her and felt the rawness of her lips? You see what she is doing to herself." Rahil sighed. "The stress will take a toll. This setup, it's not normal—we might like it, but it's not normal."

I blushed. We'd never discussed our intimate interactions with Sara before. The fact that he asked me about kissing her made me more uncomfortable than the truth. I had not only felt her rawness with my tongue. I had seen the purple-red welts on her lower lip while she was on her back, so soaked in the moments of our touching. I had grazed at her lower lip more than a couple of times in the past week, pulling it down for seconds as she moaned. My body would flinch in fright at the rippled raw punctures dotting the inside of her lower lip.

"Mira, I think it's in our best interest if we take a break for a bit."

And I started to cry. Sob. Like a teenager who had just been dumped. The pain was searing. If Ketan hadn't fucking died I wouldn't be in this ungodly situation. I would have been a mother. I would have had friends. I would have been fucking normal. I looked at Rahil. I felt like he was dying on me too. Leaving me to the world just like Ketan.

He took my glass from my hand and swallowed the remaining golden liquid. "In good time maybe we'll get a handle on things. Nobody can plan for this kind of thing, Mira. I can't risk Sara losing her health over jealousy."

"I think you're the one who can't handle it, you're the one who is jealous, and I am the one being honest. And Sara should have the courage to talk to me about this too. She gets to go on a walk while you get to be the dirty messenger? Where's your spine?"

He shrugged his shoulders at me assertively. It was his dance of power. I was in their house, he ruled it; he was the one married to Sara.

"What, are you scared that I might tell her?" The threat in my voice was unmistakable. A lioness roar. He hadn't expected it.

"Tell her what, Mira?"

"I don't know, maybe that you might be keeping her sick? That you like her like this? It must be nice to have someone sick and needing you, Rahil. You're the hero, right? You even admitted that you like having someone who needs you. You guys don't even have friends."

Rahil's body shrunk from the attack. As soon as the words were out of my mouth, I felt empty.

"I can't believe you said that."

His voice wasn't friendly. It wasn't angry either. I couldn't read him and it made me deeply uncomfortable. I had no cards left.

Perhaps they had done this before. Perhaps somewhere in this house were the remains of a broken heart, another widow who fell for their charms only to have her spirit shattered. Maybe Sara and Rahil were a team that worked together to extract all they could from vulnerable women.

He took in a noisy breath and raked his fingers through his hair. But then he came to me and let me fold half of my body onto him. "It's going to be okay," he whispered. But I had no idea what he meant. What he wanted me to do. What he was doing. Rahil was the master, but Sara was master by proxy. The easy one to blame. In the next twenty minutes Rahil repeated that he loved me and that we'd figure it out. That he was sorry for being so inconsistent and mysterious with his ways.

I was drinking a glass of water when Sara returned. She looked possessed. Happy, chatty, as if the walk had given her a new lease on life.

"I've always wanted to get out of the city, move somewhere, into the hills."

Rahil just smiled at her. "I haven't taken her on a good vacation in so long, Mira. Soon we'll go, maybe the three of us?" He looked at me, his eyes friendly, a consolation prize.

Sara nodded and said she'd love that.

"Maybe when we're old that's what we'll do, take some morphine and die quietly in Dharamshala." I winked at her.

She grabbed my hand. "Everything isn't a joke, Mira."

But her voice was cotton candy friendly, and I knew. She'd planned this. She didn't want to be the bad cop. Rahil was her messenger. She couldn't do this anymore, and I could feel it. Sara couldn't risk losing Rahil over some stupid woman she had decided to love. She could only communicate with her body.

I let my teeth graze my tongue. The water was making a weak attempt at rehydrating my whisky-dried tongue.

"So tell me, what you are teaching these days? You never talk about work."

I looked at Rahil. Sara certainly wasn't acting insecure about me being in the house. Her pretense of friendliness was grating. Rahil's eyes met mine for a second, but then he dropped his gaze to the ground, got up, and disappeared into the kitchen. So I answered, trying to remind her of the things she found so intriguing about me in the first place. I told her the latest from my world: Samina had started reading *The Second Sex* by Simone de Beauvoir and was going to talk to the class about it. It was completely off syllabus, but the students were smart and indulging them was the only hope I had for their generation.

"What's it about?"

"You've never heard of de Beauvoir?"

She shook her head, and I knew I had her. Her ignorance was always willing to award me with purpose.

What I Told Sara About *The Second Sex*

De Beauvoir disagreed with the premise that the differences between men and woman were superficial. Men and women are in fact biologically different and have experienced the world very differently. We, as women, have a very different narrative to give the world. Men and women, according to de Beauvoir, should encourage acknowledgment of these differences. But here's the important part: the reality is that men have always been "the one," the historically significant gender. They were the people who mattered, the ones who had power, choices, and agency. Women have always been "the other," the ones whose characteristics have been derived from what men are not. Women have been objects, unlike their counterparts, men, who are the subjects. Everything we've done is through the dependence on men and their agency. We've been the ones who have sculpted our existence through the needs of men. De Beauvoir didn't want a world where women were dependent on men. She just wanted both to have equal agency in the world. In essence, both are subjects and there is no room for objects.

Sara nodded along. "Yes, we are all individual souls, all of us have the ability at any time to express our individual brightness, and in this expression you'll see we are all the same one energy, Mira."

Sara could literally take any theory or opinion and bring it back to her one-soul theory. I swallowed another gulp of water. Rahil came back from the kitchen and Sara quickly filled him in on what I had said about *The Second Sex*. My heart started to beat faster. I'd had coffee the day before with Rahil, and we'd discussed the privilege of philosophy. I started to feel excited again. The three of us talking about something that I loved to talk about. The two of them anchored to my thoughts, my memories, my knowledge.

"Yeah, hah, just like you were telling me the other day, Mira. That Maslow's hierarchy of needs determines those privileged enough to debate our existence. Here we are sipping our whisky calmly, while the rest of the world goes to shit. But, oh, like Mira says, there is a place for philosophy too, even if it's privileged."

His words sliced my heart. The other day, he had nodded, even grazed my cheek with his finger, like he had understood what I had said. Now, there was something unmistakably snide in his tone. Rahil wasn't even that politically inclined or pessimistic about the world. At least not the Rahil who sipped caramel lattes with me in the evenings.

Sara shifted on the sofa, her face pulled in. "You guys met outside?"

"Yeah, Sara, for coffee. I was done with work early, I forgot to tell you," Rahil said calmly. As if it were a one-off coffee. As if it were not something we did almost weekly.

My heart shifted. Sara's tone had flattened when she had asked the question. No friendly curiosity weaved through her words. They had tricked me. They still wanted me out. I had fallen for it twice in a span of forty-five minutes. I felt a hot shame burn my forehead. And with it came a choked tongue. I no longer knew what was happening. I no longer knew what to say.

We had never said that our phone calls and our once-in-a-while meetings alone were supposed to be secrets. They were premised on an unsaid understanding: we needed each other to fuel us for Sara—for us to love Sara. Or so I'd thought. Was this now his final revenge, his way of punishing me for forcing him to share the woman (thing?) he loved the most? Or was it his way of making sure I couldn't tell Sara of my own suspicions about him?

Sara stared at Rahil for whole seconds. Then she turned to me. "I guess I am not needed as much as I thought I was."

She stood up and went into the bedroom and slammed the door shut. Her music started playing moments later. Rahil reached for his glass of whisky. He looked at me, his face twisted in smug arrogance. I was a pebble in an ocean, an insignificant dot. Tears danced in my eyes again, but I blinked them away. I wouldn't repeat the same grief I had experienced not even an hour ago with Rahil. I considered telling Sara about the oatmeal. But I already knew she wouldn't care, wouldn't even believe me. I was the enemy now.

"This is what I was trying to tell you. Her mood is just not stable, she hasn't figured out how to be in sync with this. But she wants it too at the same time."

"Yeah, and I am the one who is easiest to get rid of, aren't I?"

"There are boundaries. This is my and Sara's house first. You're just a friend, and friends have their own homes."

His voice was drained of any sentiment. So cold, for a minute I thought he was joking. He went into the bedroom, leaving me alone on the couch. I could hear his voice rise. "It's time... You show her... done to yourself... have to."

I had never heard Rahil raise his voice at Sara. I could hear Sara murmur. The door swung open, Rahil was clutching Sara's forearm. He dragged her to the living room. I wanted to pounce on him, rip him away from Sara, but I froze. Sara's eyes were lit with terror. "Show her!" Rahil demanded.

The confusion on my face was no match for the utter sorrow that washed over Sara's. I focused on Rahil's hand; it gripped her wrist so tightly it could have sliced it off. He swung Sara toward the couch; there she was, right beside me.

"She's already so sick, and what I am trying to tell you is that our situation here is inflaming it. She is so stressed, her mouth is in shreds. Show her, Sara!"

Sara's eyes were glazed with tears; her pale cheeks glowed in shame. She shook her head. "It's just that I can't handle it anymore. The nights... I keep thinking I am losing everything." She hiccupped three rapid sobs.

Rahil took in a breath. He stood in front of her and pushed her shoulders to the couch. In a split second he used his thumb and index finger to pull open her mouth. She didn't resist. She slumped as a mannequin would. "Look!" he commanded.

I looked—into the depth of her mouth. My stomach fell. The damage was much worse than I could have imagined. How had she ever kissed me back and not cried in pain? How had I never looked at her this close-ly? The insides of her cheeks were pocked with thick bubbles. Her lower lip was clotted and uneven, shriek-ing red. I put my hands to my mouth in shock. Sara final-ly pushed away Rahil's hand and disappeared into the bedroom. Rahil followed without another word to me.

I sat on the couch in silence for minutes, wishing, hoping, willing them to come back, to hug me, to tell me they loved me. They'd been wrong—we all were stron-ger than this. We didn't care what society demanded, ours was an irreplaceable bond. But no one came out. No one said those things.

I shut my eyes. I saw Ketan. Yellow shirt, beige pants. I had conquered grief, he reminded me. I had conquered uncertainty. I had jumped from the rug that had almost pulled the life I knew out from under me. Ketan's hand reached out, urging me onward. I could walk back to normal. I could walk right out and be the me I had been all this while. I didn't need Sara and Rahil. I didn't need their games. I opened my eyes. Ketan was gone.

I left their house and went straight to Appa's. I told him that the boyfriend I'd never told him about had broken up with me and he held me like a little girl. Sara's torn mouth would flash in my mind and I'd feel my stomach turn. What had I done to her? What had Rahil done to make her think I was the threat?

I spent the night there, Appa singing an old Tamil song to me. Hours later, too tired to think, I lay with my face in the pillow, inhaling the scent of my pillowcase. It reminded me of my hazy childhood—nothing delightful, nothing tragic. Just familiar.

In the morning, Appa gave me a plate of toast and fruit.

"It's a new day, it's time for you to go teach some children. Now go do what you have to do."

XIV

I went to work with a new determination. I had a mother who'd committed suicide. I had lost my husband after less than a year of marriage. I had survived, and I could push past this too. I was not weak or needy. I was not Sara, who couldn't communicate what she felt with words. Sara who needed to skip this part of her "eternal life." And I certainly wasn't a two-faced asshole like Rahil.

Mrs. Meena, the head of the physics department, asked me to help her choreograph a medley with the seventh-grade kids for Annual Day. "Hindi songs, it will be fun, and you need to do some more fun things. You are always into all that serious stuff," she squealed. She wore a bright yellow salwar kameez and a large red bindi, and had overly black-lined eyes. I couldn't help but think she looked like a bee.

I burst out laughing, shaking my head in mock protest. Truth was, it did sound fun, and helping kids dance to some stupid Hindi song was, probably, exactly what I needed.

At lunch break we gathered at the central student plaza. Samina was there, tucked into a corner of the plaza, observing the rest of us. I couldn't place her emotion, but her stare was intense. Samina was not the dancing type. She had set up a far too serious reputation among her peers to participate in something as frothy as this. I smiled at her and she raised her hand in calm acknowledgment. For a whole minute I reconsidered my decision, wondering if students like Samina would think less of me.

The music burst from the speakers. Immediately, Mrs. Meena started to demonstrate the steps for the first thirty seconds of the dance. The Hindi song was about love and breakups, but also included an original English rap:

Love it, baby, when you breakup,
My heart still says, baby,
What's it, it's okay, darling,
We'll still be together on WhatsApp.

"This song is ridiculous," I scolded over the music. Mrs. Meena looked at me sidelong, reached her hands out imploringly for me to join her. Apparently, bad rhymes could win over almost anyone, even overqualified physics teachers and morose English teachers. Two boys whom I had never taught came up to me and very sincerely asked me to start dancing so they could copy my moves.

"Those boys just have a crush on you, a pretty young teacher—what else will they do at this age?" Mrs. Meena shrugged her shoulders playfully and then continued to show the impatient boys the next set of moves, since I had stopped to watch Samina walking toward me.

"Miss Mira, you didn't reply to my email."

"Samina, I am so sorry, it's just that I have this other project I am working on at home. Did you send me the essay?"

"What else? You said it was okay if I write it just for you."

"Yes, and I need to give it the time it deserves..."

"I understand, Miss Mira." She made it easy—she didn't need excuses, she just needed me to read it. She looked over at the kids swaying to the music and then looked at me.

"You want to dance?"

"Maybe next year, miss." She finally smiled at me and walked back to her corner.

Mrs. Meena was showing the girls how to do the first eight-count steps. She pointed her hand energetically to the boys standing lackadaisically to the side. "You teach them, Mira."

In the middle of my hip thrusting I felt my phone buzz in my pocket. It was from Sara.

Mira, let us be for now.

My heart dropped, my head filled with rage. I began typing: *He's making you sick, he's the one who keeps you so unhappy. He's the one who needs you to be sick. He's the one who makes you self-harm.* But the futility of it all filled my head. Instead, I heaved my phone with demon strength across the plaza. It bounced twice and lay shattered thirty meters away.

The students gaped in awe. Mrs. Meena audibly gasped. I pulled my hands through my hair in response to the thick embarrassment that pulsed through my body. I walked with purpose toward the phone, picked it up, traced my fingers on the shattered glass, and mumbled, *"Shit, shit, shit."* I didn't have to look up to know everybody was staring.

Mrs. Meena came up to me. "Are you all right?"

I didn't answer as she stroked my head gently.

"Go home, take the rest of the day off," she cooed. "Whatever's going on will smooth out."

In that moment I wished she were my mother—the happy mother Appa had talked about. The mother who could hold me and make everything dissolve into a gentle breeze. The next second I didn't want my mother or any weird replacement of her. I wanted to be on the farm again, surrounded by shelves. I wanted my eyes and my mind locked in the safety of words written by men and women long ago. I looked up at her and nodded. As I walked toward the staff room to collect my things, I caught Samina staring at me from her corner, her eyes lingering on my body and her intense gaze piercing my back as I exited.

In the staff room another teacher told me that the principal had called me to his office. I sighed loudly. I loved my conversations with Mr. Khan, but this time I knew it wasn't casual Marxism he wanted to discuss.

"Did you eat? I have some roti and daal left." Mr. Khan was wrapping up lunch at his desk.

I waved my hands at him. "No, no, I am full, thank you."

He opened a bottle of hand sanitizer and squirted a blob out on his palm. As he rubbed, the air flooded with that clinical hospital smell. He took a deep breath in, twitched his mouth.

"The thing is, Mrs. Meena thought your help with the dance might, uh, help you. The teachers said, uh, you've been slightly off the last couple months. Not to say the students or parents have complained. But just, we care about your well-being, Mira."

"I've just been a bit distracted, that's all, Mr. Khan, really. Actually I am just pulling things together right now, and uh..."

"I heard you just threw your phone across a plaza full of kids. Scared them. I can only imagine what kind of text you must have gotten to do such a thing, but whatever it is, your personal matter, we can't..." His voice trailed. I knew he felt stupid giving me moralistic lectures like this. He was an interloper to traditional academia, and his rant was unbecoming.

"I reacted on impulse. I am sorry. This won't happen again."

"Good, and I don't think it will. Eleventh grade is enjoying your teaching, and they really have taken to history. I had Ranvir in here the other day saying how he wanted to study anthropology after school. It's because of the way you were teaching them to read. You know, feel free to teach out of syllabus. But careful, like I said, the parents do come to us from time to time with their bourgeois worries. A fine balance, Mira, a fine balance." He looked to his desk and started tapping it with his fingers.

I nodded my head, assuring Mr. Khan some more. I even used some of his hand sanitizer as I talked. He told me to go home for the day. I didn't argue. Primarily because I already had an idea of what to do next. Something that would get me back on track. I would not let five words destroy me. I was stronger than that.

I got home and flipped my laptop open. My bed was pristine, my house neat. I had barely been around in the last few months, and I had missed my sheets, the smell of the walls. That mellow, woody, earthy smell that I walked into every day. Before Sara, before the loony farm, before everything, I had friends. Ketan and I had a community of people. Not that we were overly social, but I had people to gossip with, friends from the office, friends who texted me to go to movies. Friends who would share beer and Scrabble in our living room that always smelled of sandalwood because it was the only incense Ketan would ever buy.

After he died, I still kept in touch on social media; sometimes there were even emails. But it's only now that I realized I hadn't really hung out with anyone in the last year. I hadn't really looked with curiosity at the pictures that flooded my newsfeed: babies, dogs, trips to Phi Phi Island, promotions, and anniversaries. Old colleagues smiling into their phone cameras, fancy plated dinners, and new babies on their laps. Mountains behind them, wearing dapper checkered coats on benches in Europe. Normal life and what it looked like. I chuckled mindlessly looking through, catching up, understanding what had happened to whom. The information had always been there. This gold mine of adventures and evolutions. For whole moments I couldn't get over the fact that I hadn't been compelled to sit down and read into the lives of others in so long.

I had wanted nothing of other people and their boring, predictable lives after I came back from the farm. Even less after my body was soothed in the arms of Sara.

But now it was the only thing I wanted. Talk of husband promotions and movie reviews; I wanted pregnancy stories, makeup tips, and goofy laughter. I wanted all the things from before.

There she was: Shriya, a good friend at one point. She now had a baby boy who was more than a year old. She'd become a stay-at-home mom and, by the looks of it, a well-kept one. Her dress seemed to be sharper than I remembered, back when we used to go watch movies right after work. Shriya was a good-hearted woman, innocuous enough, not above gossip, with an addiction to bad Bollywood. I scrolled through more photos. She had gotten married right after Ketan died, but I had never really met the husband, save for the time they had come over to our house to give their condolences. She was a brand-new bride then, the orange-red mehendi still fresh on her hands.

It was the last time I saw her. Her husband was handsome. I clicked on his profile. He was already a VP in a midsized organization in fintech. Her baby boy wasn't all that cute. I immediately felt bad for thinking that. Her album was filled with birthday parties and lipsticked mommies posing for selfies. Then there was an older album, from right before they had their baby, of a couples' trip to Cambodia. I hit the messenger button.

Shriya!

It's been so long. We can both blame each other, but let's just blame life. I see you have a beautiful baby boy! He is tremendously cute. I am a teacher now—weird, right? I was thinking about our movie dates today, and I thought

*I would say hi. How about we catch up this week? Let me
know.*

I hit send and closed my laptop. In between those
sentences lay days of me at the farm, days of me understanding myself again. It held secrets and sex. It held the
story of my mother. A message like this reduced me to a
shimmer of light, a passing wink.

I switched on the TV and found myself enjoying an
old rom-com from the '90s. I was enjoying it so much
that I got up midway to make popcorn. I propped my
head up with pillows, shoved popcorn down my throat,
and washed it down with an old bottle of Limca that was
lying in my fridge. I felt fucking content. Ketan, are you
seeing me now? I am happy; who knew it would take a
rom-com and popcorn?

My phone buzzed—it was messenger. Shriya had replied.

*Mira! OMG so long. What the hell, babe? How is your
father? Teacher! That's crazy. Listen, I am going to my parents' home in Delhi for a month, we're celebrating their fiftieth
anniversary. Full family and all. I'll message you when I am
back. Promise.*

A whole month before Shriya could distract me. I
was still buzzing from the movie. Undaunted, I scrolled
my newsfeed, looking out for those faces from the past.
There were 456 to choose from.

XV

I am only human.

I admit there were days I plotted. I toyed with the idea of playing detective. I could and would find out the truth about Sara and Rahil. I could and would understand my role in their lives. I could make Sara love me again.

But I didn't. I could barely sleep at night; my hands would scroll down my phone into the early hours of the morning. Al Jazeera, BBC—the rest of the world was there for company and offered unadulterated friendship. I drank too much coffee in the mornings, but it worked. I was open, my mouth swollen with conversation, teaching, discussing, telling kids to shut up in the back seats.

I had Appa too, and he didn't make a scene of me visiting him more often now that I was "single" again. He didn't ask questions about my mysterious boyfriend; he didn't care for those details. He was all about Indonesian history these days. He was mad and upset with pop history, specifically because it didn't seem concerned with recording enough about some of the world's most gruesome genocides. Appa's words and opinions kept me in a sort of coma, a calm waking sleep I was happy to accept.

What Appa Told Me About
the Indonesian Genocide

On October 1, 1965, six generals from the Indonesian army were killed; the blame was put squarely on the communists. And overnight there was a violent outrage against them. "The Chinese people of Indonesia, the perceived 'leftists,' they were about to endure their own holocaust," Appa said as he dunked a crisp piece of dosa into coriander chutney. The bloodbath lasted a year. "I say more than a million died. You'll see half that number in some places, but do your research, there were bodies piled everywhere.

"The world was already at the height of communist paranoia. It was in the middle of the Cold War and Lyndon B. Johnson was president. America played a great role in encouraging the Indonesian army to seek out communists, even funding them," he said with the confidence only book memory could give you. "Bah, the average American wouldn't know where Indonesia is on a map, much less their own country's involvement in about a hundred wars, forget genocide."

By the third meeting with Appa, his obsession with genocide had turned personal: "In my day, we didn't have the internet, but we could locate Poland, Chicago, and Laos on a map, and we could tell you about the pros and cons of Kennedy, even Eisenhower. Mind you, Mira, that's besides all the things we knew about our own country."

I had nodded my head in support. Had it been last year, I would have felt the same level of rage Appa had for the uninformed world. But now, I could only pretend to feel the same way. Appa went on relentlessly. "But no, now this generation of kids you teach, they are going the zombie American way, little bubbles where they can't make any kind of historical connections. Fascism and Big Brother will smack them on their heads, and they won't know what hit them. In fact, they'll go running into its attractive, commercial arms."

He wasn't getting the same conviction from me. I wasn't the girl he had grown to admire. The girl who read, the girl who knew it all. The girl who could dissect the world and its injustices. It must have punched him in the gut, my stoic response. My utter lack of passion.

I considered being swayed by Appa's current bag of apples, to go full force in the classroom with the un-known horrors Indonesia had suffered. Maybe Samina's class would enjoy it; they by far had the best disposition to withstand old-school intellectual banter. I felt tired at the very thought of having to tell a class of students about genocide in Indonesia. Nothing close to it was in their textbooks, except for the Cold War. I said as much to Appa.

"What more do you want to connect it to? Tie it in with the stupid Cold War, that is the perfect segue. That's how you make them think."

I nodded. But I shouldn't have, because it only en-couraged him to start talking about Bangladesh. How our textbooks didn't cover the 1971 genocide nearly enough, even though it was Indian history. By that point, I realized Appa and I were having separate conversa-tions. My responses were only further burying the genocides, injustices, and victories that Appa was harping on. The world started to spin on the axis of everything unknown, a helpless drowning that made me want to go to class the next day and teach something mind-numbingly safe, like *Gulliver's Travels*.

Occasionally, I tried thinking about Samina. The idea of her always allowed me to flicker with purpose. I could be that special mentor in that gifted child's life. But this time no flicker of purpose kicked in my gut. Something achingly juvenile was happening to me—Appa's need to confront the world at large only defined my own problems with distinct clarity. I had no room in my heart for the hurt and injustice the world had felt. Appa was pushing me more toward the need to meddle with Sara and Rahil in some form. Stalking them on social media was no good. Sara didn't use it and Rahil's was a corpse feed, a rolling scroll of never-ending happy birthdays from previous years.

It was a Saturday and I had hours and hours in front of me. They hung limply from my ceiling, challenging me to get out of bed. Appa had called, but I had made up a school meeting. I considered watching YouTube videos, but the thought made my body ache with boredom. I longed for the hum of Sara's music, the sway of her body and mine. But when I shut my eyes there was only rage.

The mind can get on the highway to depression in a series of clinically predictable steps. First it is lured by the safe neatness that comes with not engaging with the everyday. Then boredom starts to crawl at the edges of the neck into the ears. *Poke, tickle, flap.* Then there's the hum of nothing, the hum of everything. That's precisely when the mind deep dives to the place where static sadness and a heavy chest are a permanent reality. I had to act fast.

I can't remember how I got there, no matter how hard I try. Why bother, though? It's inconsequential to what I ended up doing. All I remember is that I found myself at the steps of the hospital again. The swish of the automatic doors pushed away the thick humidity of the city. In the middle of the hospital's marbled floor was a giant Ganesha idol decked with layers of jasmine and marigold garlands.

Sara's words from months ago came to me: *It doesn't matter what symbol of hope you take, all that matters is what you believe.*

How many pujas had my mother offered to Ganesha, asking him to remove her crushing sense of numbness? It didn't matter. All that mattered was what I believed. Ganesha, the destroyer of obstacles, his trunk confidently snaking down his chest all the way to his full tummy. Here he was, gold-plated with the excesses of corporate hospital income. There were a few people standing around the statue, their hands in devoted prayer. I felt shame tickle my throat as I imagined their sick family members, currently admitted in this very hospital. And here I was praying for my love story to be less complicated. But the shame didn't last in my body, and I had to stop myself from lecturing the older lady wearing a south silk sari that no prayer could stop the body from dying if it needed to. Instead I walked toward the help desk and asked a uniformed woman how I could make an appointment with Dr. Mudra.

"You should have made an appointment, he is very busy. You can do a walk-in, but you'll have to wait. No guarantees. Third floor, walk past general surgery and orthopedics."

I waited after informing the desk nurse that I was a "walk-in." She looked at me and frowned, scribbling something onto her clipboard while sticking out her left hand, signaling me to sit down. The air-conditioning was far too cold, and goose bumps sprung all over my arms as I held myself tightly, legs swinging back and forth. At least I looked like a wreck—maybe I would get in after all. There seemed to be four patients ahead of me and all of them had a friend or a spouse with them. One woman had her head on her husband's shoulder. He looked dully into his cell phone. His work badge was cradled in bunches of fabric that had collected near his stomach. I wondered why a man like that had bought and worn a formal shirt that was at least two sizes too big. I knew that I was wondering about it only because I didn't want to acknowledge the truth. What I wanted was the shoulder of someone as regular as that guy. Even if he was some boring cell-phone-addicted man who couldn't get his shirt size right.

The thick wooden door opened and a patient walked out. As the door started to close by itself, I saw Dr. Mudra sitting behind his pristine white desk. His eyes focused on me. The nurse was motioning to the oversized shirt guy to take his wife in next. But the nurse's phone rang, and then she looked over to me, her face disapproving.

"After this couple you can go next."

He had seen me. He wanted to talk to me. I was going to get the information I wanted. I chanted this to myself for twenty minutes. Finally, the nurse snapped her fingers and waved to me to go inside. I rubbed my arms, trying to will the goose bumps away.

Dr. Mudra was trying hard to look serious. It was the way his mouth twitched. I remembered it being kinder looking when I had met him in the cafeteria. Today he wore a somber maroon shirt buttoned all the way to the top.

"You are Sara's friend, aren't you?"

I nodded and took a seat right opposite him. His face lit up in a smile for the first time. "Well, the patient chair is right here." He pointed to the chair closer to him.

"I won't take much of your time—I'm just trying to get some answers." My own confidence and clear articulation almost threw me off track, but I pressed on. "Supposing I wanted to, uh, help myself, and I was aware of certain things that I am doing—would you be able to give me an educated guess on your thoughts?"

"Why do I get the impression you are looking for a psych evaluation? You know well I am a neurologist."

"Please, Dr. Mudra."

His eyes softened. He took off his brown glasses and cupped his chin in his palms. He had surrendered to me, I could feel it.

"I am just looking to see what I could have—you know, if I feel sick all the time, and, you know, if I've even somehow managed to bring on seizures, even though all my tests are normal, would you call me a hypochondriac? What would you call me?"

Dr. Mudra inhaled deeply. I could feel his professional resistance. I could also feel his need to spill the beans.

"Well, I don't think stringent labels help anyone," he said finally. Disappointment began to pool in my gut. He cleared his throat. "But the mind is a powerful thing. Are you honestly trying to help—" He paused and sniffed. "Help yourself?"

I nodded vigorously.

"The mind is a powerful thing, sometimes I think we haven't even begun to understand its powers."

I bit my lip. I had him on my leash, but he was tugging me the other way. He was sounding more like Sara. "I know that, but in our capacity as it stands, what do you think I should look into?"

He studied me for one long, hard moment. I sat frozen, waiting for the payoff.

"I think you should look into something called Munchausen syndrome. And a person taking care of such a person, well, they don't know what to do anymore apart from accepting it."

I repeated the words back to him, begging him with my tone to tell me more.

"And really, that's all I can say. You've cut other patients' place in line, so I'd appreciate it if you would get going and get yourself to a doctor who works with the mind for a living."

This was as good as it was going to get. I leaped out of my seat and took one last look at him. His eyes were sad.

XVI

I chanted "Munchausen syndrome" the entire way back in the auto-rickshaw. I held off searching for the term on my phone, wanting to be fully in control, on my computer. The term felt familiar. Had Oprah said something about it? Had I read something about it?

I read every medical definition first. I nourished every new link and click with sips of chamomile. I could feel Sara in me, I could feel her breath grazing the back of my shoulder. I could feel her sense of betrayal as I read more and more, my eyes squinting into the glow of my computer screen.

Munchausen was rarely diagnosed in India. The internet defined it to me over and over again: a need to be surrounded by all things medical and an obsession over failing health. For someone with Munchausen—otherwise known as factitious disorder—doctors, medical tests, and subsequent attention are akin to that of a loving parent. Think of a child needing this loving parent all the time, but the child is always ignored because, well, the child is healthy. But this child must be with its damn parent somehow, so the mind and body find a way. The mind convinces itself of the body's failing. The body, burdened by the mind, is ultimately weakened and submits.

I read about borderline personality, something that seemed to merge with Munchausen. I ticked the symptoms I thought Sara had: chronic feelings of emptiness, paranoia, fear of abandonment, impulsive anger. It occurred to me I had them all too. Goddamn labels. As far as I could tell, everyone was a fucking borderline personality.

Camus's *The Stranger* stared at me from my wooden coffee table. The book lay on the table so calmly, it talked to me. *Mira, here lies your past life, you've forgotten what it means to be you.* I felt no regret. Once again, I went to Google. Before, books had created an intellectual barrier. I had taught myself not to succumb to the hyperbole of Western science and labeling, the instant gratification of having all the answers at one's fingertips. But now it was all I had.

It wasn't enough to understand Sara, far from it. The bullet point symptoms did not cover her laugh, her attachment to the soul, her disdain for reality, her musky rose scent, her contemplative chamomile sips. I read an article about a child whose mother suffered from Munchausen by proxy, dragging her child to doctors and watching as her child was subjected to three unnecessary surgeries. The mother, the author deduced in retrospect, found her safety in doctors, a safety she had missed as a child when her own father had died. It didn't add up, not in Sara's case. Plus, Sara was so self-aware, so blatant about the mind and so sure of her soul. Yes, Sara had protective parents, but all her symptoms didn't tie up well to this narrative. No, her DNA was knitting her consciousness in a new direction, one that had to destroy itself first before it could rise. I was sure of it. The only thing I was sure of.

Rahil wasn't making her sick. He was just complicit in it. He deserved his own term. Munchausen by complacency. Munchausen by the exotic thrill that comes with caring for such beautiful destruction.

On the second night of research, I discovered a forum where Munchausen sufferers spilled their darkest feelings. I added myself as a user and spent the entire night on the forum, scrolling by every comment, excited that I had so much content to stay with me for the night. The users were primarily from America:

I am thirty-seven years old, been suffering from factitious disorder for the last decade. At my worst I was injecting insulin from my dad's supply so that my blood sugar levels were low in tests. I never got treated, diagnosed myself.

No one really suspects anything. I spend most of my time reading medical journals. I am studying to become a certified nursing assistant. I guess working in that environment might help me from just being the patient? Don't laugh, please.

I cut my thumb at an urgent care and put it in my urine cup so I could show my doctor I had blood in my urine. They are treating me for a UTI now, but they sent me home. I don't know what to do most days.

They think it's stress. And it is stress! Stress that I want the doctor to think there is something really, really physically wrong. Stress that I want him to do something serious about it. But when they diagnose "stress," they just ask me to do breathing exercises, and I get nothing. I walk out empty-handed. So frustrating. And alone. Anyone else feeling me?

I am older than you, but high school was a disaster. I had my tonsils out because I basically demanded the doctor take them out of me. Hang in there.

When you're ready, go to therapy, get help. Admitting the problem is embarrassing. But it's not worth it to live like that. I am not 100 percent yet myself, maybe I'll never be, but I am better now.

All the comments essentially same. Then I stopped. It was very late at this point, nearing dawn.

Yello1996: Anyone ever fake a seizure?

@ yello1996: Totally! It used to be my go-to illness before I got myself some help (okay, well, before I finally got caught by one of my doctors). I used to fake them in high school and even in college. I'd even wet myself for authenticity. It got me a ton of hospital visits and a bunch of attention from my family and friends. But I wasn't smart enough to demonstrate the aftereffects of it: confusion, disorientation, lethargy. I was too high off adrenaline with the attention. One doctor caught on years later, though, asked me a bunch of personal questions. I was diagnosed with BPD and then factitious disorder. My family are naturally attention-giving when something is wrong, so even this diagnosis got them worried and I was happy, I mean whatever gives me that high. But then I had to do the work and try to get better. It's like being a chain-smoker who has to quit. You can quit, but you'll always want one. I feel you, but resist, you could get yourself killed with unnecessary meds.

There is something reassuring about the clipped but friendly confessions of Americans online, a quality I suspect the rest of the world admires as well. It's the blunt ability to share their most private vulnerabilities, while dutifully sticking to categories and the confines of defined symptoms. There is something deeply myopic about it too.

Yet here they were, sprawling clinical testimonials that matched Sara's behaviors. There was every logical reason to apply these testimonials to Sara's life and diagnose her unquestionably. But I could see Sara rolling her eyes and only making me feel stupid. I could see Sara looking at me and shaking her head for believing in medical labels.

But then I remembered how Sara acted after we had run toward her in the park. How she'd stopped shaking and sat up. She was weak for a few minutes, but her eyes, they were bright. Come to think of it, Sara's eyes always seemed bright. Even when she complained of dulling cramps and aching knees. And then there was her ability to talk to me in detail about her day even though she claimed she had a pounding headache. The first day I had met her, I was for all practical purposes a new person who had seen her being ill. *A new person to perform for.* Rahil was happy too, more so than his usual temperament, as I've come to know it. It was almost like he was feeding off her adrenaline rush too.

They're both sick little insects, I thought. Heartbreak comes in waves, and now it had flooded my entire body. I turned on a Turkish Sufi song on YouTube and I found myself headed toward my bedroom. I sat on the corner of my mattress and pretended Sara was next to me, that we were swaying together. But when I closed my eyes I saw Ketan. He was smiling, yellow shirt, khaki pants.

You got so much more to do, Mir-Mir.

It sounded so real, my eyes blinked open. I felt terror at first, and then I just felt lonely.

XVII

I resurrected two more people from my past. The first was Shomon, a Bengali classmate I had gone to school with until twelfth grade. The second was Asha, a colleague I used to work with when I was in communications. She had worked under Ketan and used to be the single girl who went to all the parties. Now her social media told another story. Just like Shriya, she too had a young toddler and was living the Indian urban mommyhood dream. Shomon, however, was clearly single.

I met Shomon on a Saturday. He had recently divorced; his wife had wanted to live in Kolkata, where her family was. But career opportunities had brought him to Suryam.

"It's the new Indian divorce, we don't understand compromise," he said, sipping a cappuccino, the froth bubbling on his mustache.

His very presence irritated me from the start. I couldn't really justify my annoyance, so I flip-flopped between aggressive, challenging comments and sickly-sweet encouraging phrases that only served to confuse the poor man.

"Well, if you guys were really in love, wouldn't you have found a way?" I dipped my hand into my empty cup, scooping up a wet lump of undissolved sugar. He cringed. I couldn't tell at first if it was because of the sugar on my finger or because of my remark.

He giggled in nervousness. "Yeah, maybe, but we'd known each other since college, what can I say? We both were unhappy, but don't you think running away back to your family is childish? Life brings change, she should have looked forward to a new city."

"We've got the Rasagura, not much else. Kolkata has far more personality."

Shomon knew about Ketan's death, though he had never met him. He used the fact that both of us were single to unabashedly suggest us meeting more. "I like women like you—strong and independent."

I liked that men felt compelled to say things like this these days. I wondered how he would have truly felt if I had told him the truth. *I'm in love with a married woman, and I kind of have a relationship with her husband too. They've gotten really mad at me, and I haven't seen them in weeks. My heart is literally being stomped on. And guess what else? The woman I love has a rare mental illness, one that I can guarantee you've never heard of. It's worse than losing a husband seven months into a marriage. A husband whom I very much loved.*

I imagined him either jumping to his feet and leaving the café in confusion, or just plain laughing at me. But I said none of this. Instead, I told him about teaching, I told him about genocide and how schools don't cover it enough in history class.

"Serious topics—don't be so serious. You've been so strong already."

Of course I wanted to slap him the moment he said that. But I have a tendency to smile when a person out-shines my preconceived notions of his stupidity. Shomon tried another line of engagement. Nostalgia. School days, stained uniforms, the scary math teacher, and how we cheated in physics, because the teacher pretty much allowed it. I let him go on. As he talked he mentioned we should go out for a stroll and I shrugged indifferent-ly—it didn't matter if we were sitting or walking, my experience of Shomon was going to be the same. He paid the bill for two coffees, 511 rupees, with exact change, stunning the barista, who raised her thick eyebrows in appreciation. As we stepped out into the muggy sun, his hand tried to graze mine. He pointed to the other side of the road where the sidewalk extended without any breaks for at least a kilometer. All the trendy pubs were lined up there, and as we crossed the road Shomon very confidently took my hand. Nothing like a chaotic street filled with scooters, mopeds, cars, and auto-rickshaws to enhance his confidence. I let my hand stay in his hand. I don't know why—maybe it was to remember what it felt like.

He was still talking about the past by the time we were on the nicer sidewalk. I even interjected with a few random (and mostly made up) memories I had that dovetailed with his recollections.

We sidestepped a large crow pecking at a bloated rat carcass on the sidewalk and weaved in and out of weekend crowds, mostly hip kids in their early twenties waiting for the last of their friends before they entered pubs that would serve them brunch, strawberry-flavored liqueurs, and gin on ice. Their expensive perfume inflated in my nostrils: juicy apple, magnolia, lily rose, earthy cotton, and sandalwood. We walked aimlessly through all of it.

On the ledge outside a coffee shop I finally sat down. A black-spotted stray looked at me, his ears perked up on eye contact. Ketan had had a thing for dogs, especially the ones on the roads. His mother used to feed strays in the evenings when he was growing up. I was always weary of them, but Ketan always called to them like they were his own, making kissing sounds and petting them. Today I felt Ketan in me. I put my hand out to the unusually inquisitive stray. It came right over to me, tail wagging; Shomon moved inches away in fright. The dog got up on its hind legs in excitement and placed his front paws on my knees. I stroked the dog and felt an odd sense of love for it.

"They carry diseases, you shouldn't touch them."

I bit my lip in irritation and shrugged, continuing to pet the dog.

None of this derailed Shomon, though. He didn't want the date to end and asked if we should go to a movie. I told him I had to take my father to the doctor, which was a complete lie, but one that quickly gets you out of any social commitment. "We'll meet next week," I said, although I had no intention of ever talking to him again.

For the next few days Shomon WhatsApp-ed me: *sup, howz ur day? saturday night movie?* He also forwarded a slew of sexist wife-husband jokes with crying-laughing emojis. I finally blocked his number after I received a message from him at midnight: *so nice 2 connect with u after all dis time, weird, but i already miss you.*

I also blocked him on social media and felt like a cruel bitch. I worried about karma and how my unkindness would retaliate in the form of more heartbreak. But really, I didn't care.

I ordered a bunch of books, the same books that had surrounded me on the farm: de Beauvoir, Sartre, Camus, Foucault, even Chomsky for good measure. Looking at the books on Amazon had made my heart swell with old familiarity and a sense of impending safety. Just the thought of the books made me feel like I could get through it all, just forget Sara and Rahil. I'd exist solely for the questions Sartre asked.

I met Asha a few days after blocking Shomon. (Good thing they weren't connected at all, but then, I wouldn't have cared anyway.) She invited me to her house to meet her two-year-old, Simran, whom she'd named after the protagonist in the '90s blockbuster *Dilwale Dulhania Le Jayenge*.

"Retro," I had managed when she first told me.

She had the quintessential I've-married-into-prime-upper-middle-class apartment. Three large bedrooms and two gigantic verandas, one overlooking the apartment pool and the other over the apartment dog park.

"Simran loves doggies, we go every evening to watch Bongo and Sha-Sha, don't we, Simmy?"

Her husband was in the United States for a two-week project management gig.

"So cold in Boston, it's all he can talk about. In fact I told him, 'Why don't you go to an American strip club to get warmed up?' We like to joke like that. We're, like, best friends."

I managed not to cringe. I picked up Simran, who immediately burst into tears. Asha shook a stuffed frog at her and her hands flung toward the toy. She took her frog and walked to the other side of the room. "Let her be with that frog, now we can talk."

We sat in the living room for hours. She had laid out samosas, sliced apples, and Rasagura. We drank an Indian red wine from her friend's estate. She didn't really ask me about my life; instead she concerned herself with my next marriage.

"You need to stop this, you are so young, there are so many men out there, and really, once you settle down, everything is great. I mean, I actively chose to be a mother to Simran, but if you want to work too, there is no harm."

She fished out her phone.

"Look," she said, her eyes lit up with sudden mischief. "You need to get on this app, all the men in the world—well, in this city at least—and you can find out from the very start if they are smart and successful or not."

I burst out laughing. "Why are you on it? You're married."

"Oh! It's just for fun, Akash knows all about it—you know, it's good to flirt once in a while. I show him all my chats."

I stopped laughing. I looked at her profile description. *Here to let new friendships bloom. Movie addict, Ex-HR back-*

ground. Music fanatic. She had three pictures on it: one with her in sunglasses with a very fresh-looking mojito, the second with one leg propped on a giant red wall, like a movie heroine, and the third an "au naturel" selfie. I scrolled past them with frantic interest, with disgust, with thrill. A little fly of judgment started to buzz around my head, then turned into a wasp, stinging, pleading with me: tell this woman she is an idiot and walk out. But my mind fought back; it told me that judgment itself was ironic, irrelevant, and would only make me the stupid one. Instead I let compassion rise. Maybe she was lonely. Akash traveled two weeks every month. Plus, I was in no position to judge, since until very recently I'd been fucking a mentally ill married woman and her husband to boot.

She tried to set up a profile for me, but I promised I'd do it myself when I felt ready. Her face fell, but she nodded understandingly. "Yes, you must be ready, but remember, schoolchildren can give you happiness, but it will be your own that will give you the most joy."

I looked at Simran in the corner, who was still fiddling with the frog. I couldn't help but think about the children I could have had with Ketan. Simran looked up and met my eye. Maybe Asha was right.

I found myself nodding to an invitation to Asha's fourth wedding anniversary party at the Hyatt. It was another thing to distract me and I was willing to take anything.

By the end of the third week of my separation from Sara and Rahil, I was back on top of my teaching game and the other teachers had stopped swarming me with concerned glances. The classroom had lost a chunk of spark, though. Samina had dengue. She was devastated that she couldn't give her presentation on *The Second Sex*. I read her email twice, savoring the weird nature of this girl in all her tortured glory:

Hi, Miss Mira,

I had everything ready, even a PowerPoint. But Mom insists I recover at home and even do homeschooling for a month. I guess I'll give it another read and maybe do something way more powerful. I have a few ideas. I'll be back in January for sure.

Please don't do anything fun before I am back.

Hugs!

Samina

P.S. You still haven't read my Hitler essay, have you, miss?

Meanwhile, the books I'd ordered had started trickling in. I began flipping through them, but something was missing and I quickly set them down. All that kept me secure in the evenings were memories of my first and last times in bed with Rahil, talking about Sara. Our shared love for this woman. Now my nights were filled with olfactory hallucinations—her rosy musk, her sweat. I heard her music in my head too, so vivid it would wake me up in the middle of the night. I would charge to the kitchen to make a cup of chamomile. I'd pick up a book, read a page, and then picture Sara laughing at it. *All your men and their lofty thoughts*, I could hear her saying. I wanted to show her Asha's dating profile, I wanted to

tell her about Simran's frog. I longed for the sound of
Rahil walking through the front door at six o'clock. I inhaled deeply and swore I smelled Sara.

XVIII

Another month went by, both slowly and fast. I even managed to go to Asha's anniversary party. Her husband looked like a Punjabi pop star playboy. He was nice enough, but I couldn't imagine him being faithful to Asha. He even tried to flirt with me. I had given them a set of books, the ones I had ordered from Amazon. It was my own inside joke. I never saw them again, but I often wondered what they'd done when they opened the box of books, all existentialism and radical politics. Maybe Akash wasn't as one-dimensional as he looked; maybe he'd read them. Maybe Asha read them sitting next to Simran and her frog. But mostly I imagined them scrunching their faces, pitying me and my life, and throwing the books out. All these scenarios gave me some unknown pleasure.

I cooked elaborate meals but didn't eat them. I watched cheesy romantic comedies after school and sometimes I researched facts on Appa's obsession: Indonesia, Bangladesh, and the communists in general. And I still spent a lot of time on factitious disorder forums in the evenings.

At the end of December, Appa and I toasted the New Year with a bottle of sparkling wine at a hill station six hours away from Suryam. We stayed in the middle of a tea estate, very much like the place my parents had come to when my mother was pregnant with me.

We were sitting by a bonfire that the staff had excited-ly put together. The heat pushed my body to the ground; it embraced me in meditative calm. The roughness of the dry mud and the poke of small rocks at my scalp felt good. By then, Appa had stopped talking about history. It was almost midnight when he coughed in preparation for a sentence that I knew he had revised in his head a few times.

"Happiness is such a subjective thing, yet it's the only thing parents want for their children. How do you calm this need without knowing what it even means to your child?"

It was the most personal thing he had said to me in a long time. He was trying. He needed intellectual reason-ing to start a fatherly conversation. It made me ache with guilt for the times I'd made up a meeting or failed to call him over the past few months.

"You could say the same thing for children—we want our parents happy."

"And I am, Mir-Mir, I've found a beautiful reliability and purpose in my life. It's you I worry about. I don't need you to tell me everything. I just need to make sure you talk to yourself, that you tell yourself everything honestly and examine it. You know your mother would have been proud of you—"

And that's where the authenticity of what he was saying failed. My mother was unknowable. My mother hadn't bothered to wait around to see if I'd make her proud. What she would have been proud of was a mystery. I didn't say as much. This was his way of apologizing for keeping such profound secrets from me. I sat back up and moved closer to him. I held Appa's hand and swallowed my lower lip.

"I can tell you that I am being more and more honest with myself every day. I can tell you that sometimes I get visions of Ketan. They used to make me sad. But now it's like he is just telling me to live. Not just live, but thrive."

Appa nodded his head in response. We heard drunken hooting rising and falling in the hills. It was midnight and Appa already had the bottle opened. "It's a screw-cap version, that cork is just nonsense, I tell you."

We each drank two small cups of sparkling wine as Appa told me stories from his days in college. None of them was particularly funny, but I responded with laughter. For two hours I managed to forget about my past. It was just Appa, me, a bonfire, and the tart sharpness of the wine.

I guess it's easy for time to go by when heartbreak gives you a predictable schedule of new habits to follow. But by now I realized I was in purgatory. Sara was too weak to make a choice, Rahil probably even more so. I had to make it for them. For myself. For my sanity. Sara had once told me if you surrender to the divine with your intent, the world around you will give you the tools.

Samina was back when school started after the New Year. On Monday she came to my desk asking when she could make her presentation. Her eyes were shining bright with such a potent excitement that I felt a rising need to crush it. But this time I was aware of my envy. It was the girl's ability to be happy with purpose alone, her ability to feel content and driven by something purely academic. Samina didn't need anyone else, certainly not the crutch of two lovers. It may have been self-centered, but standing in front of me, she also made me feel old, sloppy, and immature

"Let me see it first at break, and you can present in the afternoon grammar class."

She swung her long braid to her other shoulder and nodded her head. I found myself distracted by the shine of her hair. Envy crept up my gut again, twisting and curling around her youth.

Samina and I went into the media room since it was always empty during break. She opened her laptop. Her introductory words snapped me to attention, echoes of the writers and thoughts that lived in my own past.

"'The body is not a thing, it is a situation: it is our grasp on the world and our sketch of our project.'"

I was excited to hear de Beauvoir's ideas uttered out loud by Samina. And it wasn't because of the familiarity. I could feel something reckless forming in my head as we went through her presentation. But then I asked her the hard questions, ones that challenged her purpose. Questions that were coming from a place of an emerging agenda, but ones maybe I'd have asked years ago from a place of philosophy.

"You're right, Miss Mira, it has to be much more."

Samina. Shiny bright eyes. Shiny hair. The tools were always there. Now I knew how to use them.

I felt steady and calm going back home that evening. It changed the second I flung my door open. I looked at the empty living room and my heart disintegrated and fell to my stomach like sand. I thought about the last two months—all I had done and all I had reworked about my existence. It didn't matter, I realized. I stared at the sofa Rahil and I had had sex on. I didn't want to be alone anymore. I had played a game with myself and lost. I didn't change out of my clothes. I went to bed and pulled the blanket over my head. It was stifling, but it's what I needed.

The next day I ate a peanut butter sandwich for breakfast. It was dry and my mouth grew achy just chewing. It was as if I had already started grieving the loss of my old limitations and abilities. Yes, it was scary. But on an instinctive level I knew this had to be the next step. The afternoon brought Samina's presentation. I nodded and she came to the front of the class. Her hair was tied in a high bun. She smacked her hands together in a muted clap and glanced at me quickly: "It's more performative this time."

Her eyes lit up. She reminded me of Sara for a second. The class settled down as soon as Samina authoritatively stood at the front of the room, her hands clasped together at the middle of her chest. Her face was calm but serious. The boys in particular shut up, then shifted in their seats, unable to get comfortable.

"I am not here to do a boring book review, but rather to show you how a book needs to be represented in today's world. But, guys, I think we need to all thank Miss Mira here, for giving us insights and freedom no other teacher would."

I rolled my eyes, but I'd be lying if I said my heart didn't swell the littlest bit. The class hooted. Some boys from the back shouted, "Miss Mira rocks!"

"All right, enough guys, let's get to what Samina has to say."

Samina cleared her throat. She straightened her navy-blue uniform skirt.

"We've been taught to see this world in black and white. Some of you might think feminism means complete equality. But in *The Second Sex*, de Beauvoir actually thinks men and women are different. She says we should appreciate our different perspectives about the world. But we need to stop basing the woman's perspective off the man's. I can only show you this, not explain it to you."

The class literally leaned in together. I tilted my own head, fascinated. She had no props with her. Samina put her hand to her chest, then moved it to her collar.

"For example, the female breast, created to feed and nurture a baby, has been used as an object of sexual pleasure by patriarchy. It makes me feel like my own body must play to the tune of what an attractive breast must be like, what it must look like, instead of the functional purpose it was meant to serve. That's why I am going to ask you to try to look at me without your conditioning, just for a few seconds."

I bit my lip, instinctively feeling a pressing need to tell her to sit down, but also wanting her to go on. The class was pin-drop silent.

"Now, if you'll bear with me, imagine my breasts to be two sacks of flesh. Take away the hidden lust you might have; girls, resist the urge to compare them with yours or to judge them on the basis of what patriarchy has told you is acceptable."

My heart was beating fast. I snuck a quick peek at the other students: their eyes were glazed, hypnotized by her words. The silence in the room was a vacuum, sucking us all toward the inevitable.

Samina opened her collar button. I moved my leg out from under the desk, my head telling me to leap out at her. But some other force had me pinned to my seat. The fact that it was my fault only pressed my thighs more firmly to my chair.

She opened her second and third buttons, her cleavage spilled; her breasts were large. Her black bra showed and her fingers quickly went toward the edge of her bra. In one swift second she pulled it down to reveal her left breast.

The class was silent. But I could hear the frenzy of the students' minds.

I stood up. This would be enough for the class to report me. But before anything else could happen I heard a voice shrieking.

"Samina! What the hell are you doing?"

Mrs. Meena: my colleague was charging into the classroom and pulling the now yelling Samina, still exposed, out of the class.

"What exactly is happening in your classroom?" she spat as she hauled Samina off and away. My eyes filled with tears. I looked back at the class. They look at me helplessly, begging me for a response. The tears dried up and I started to giggle. The class joined in, a steady rising beat of uncontrollable laughter.

"I am not sure what to say, or what you all are thinking," I said when the laughter died suddenly. "I am leaving the classroom now. Please just go back to your own notes for the rest of the class period."

I trotted out of class like an animal freed from a cage, my heart pounding, both with exhilaration and mounting fear. I wondered how long Mrs. Meena had been watching. Had she been waiting to pounce? Or had she really just happened to walk by at the very moment Samina pulled her bra down?

I looked down at my phone. I had to do it now. I texted Rahil.

I am coming to your house. Back to you and Sara.

What I couldn't say in months came easily now. Effortless. Why had I never had this confidence before? When I looked up, I saw Mrs. Meena standing outside the staff room, hands folded over her mustard sari. I scuttled toward her. "Mrs. Meena, listen, I can explain about Samina, but right now, there is an emergency, my father is in the hospital."

Her mouth hung open in shock. The anger stayed thick on her face as I rushed past her and out the school gates. I felt reckless, heartless, idiotic, scampering toward the first auto-rickshaw I saw. The driver flicked his hands toward the back seat. I sat inside.

"So happy you look, madam?" the auto-driver lazily noted.

I beamed at him through his circular rearview mirror. My reflection, an ugly monster, stared back.

XIX

As the auto-rickshaw turned onto their lane, my head flushed with a kind of euphoria I suspect many would kill to feel again.

But even before we had come to a full stop, my eye had caught the lock on their gate and my heart sunk to the dusty tar of the road. The auto-rickshaw driver cleared his throat and looked at me from the rearview mirror again. I stumbled out, too embarrassed to tell him to take me home. For fifteen minutes, I paced from one side of the gate to the other, pretending this moment wasn't happening. Panic was knotting up inside me, and my muscles with it. I awkwardly walked to the gate and fumbled with the lock to check if it was really secure. Of course it was. I could feel a pressure building in my head. They had gone. They had left. Forever. It was my body that responded first. It shuddered and let out a long ache. A fierce throb that radiated to the back of my calves, the length of my neck, the edges of my fingers. I couldn't let the reality of it hit me. Yet. These were the thick seconds of non-thought I knew were vital for my preservation.

My phone buzzed. I'd forgotten it was even there. But the text had come in. A response to mine: *Mira, Sara is in the hospital.*

Sara lay like a sunken ship in the hospital bed. He hovered around her while whispering to a nurse. The staff must have applauded Rahil's dedication to his wife. It was so easy for him to play the concerned husband for the world. So easy for him to shrug off my contributions, discarding the fact that they both had needed me once.

He turned and saw me by the door.

"Mira, come in, come in," he said.

I went straight to Sara. Her hair was slick and pasted to the side of her left cheek. I traced the outline of her chin.

"Mira?" Her eyes opened in one smooth blink. "Oh, Mira. Are you okay?"

My heart leaped, and I had to control every muscle in my arms and fingers. I couldn't overreact. Perhaps I really did look like shit.

"I don't have a job anymore," I admitted.

My eyes threatened tears. But I couldn't look helpless. Or lovesick. I felt a buzzing power rising in my head as Sara gazed back, greedily, waiting for more, more of me. Rahil interjected: "She's had three seizures in the last two months, now they are running tests. She's fine now, just needs rest."

I backed away from the bed. But I didn't meet Rahil's eye. I wouldn't let him have the satisfaction of making this about her. Sara stuck out her arm in protest. "No, no, Mira, come here, don't go, I am fine, I am sick of sleeping."

I saw the hint of brightness in her eyes, but it died just as suddenly. She really was fatigued, but also at peace, finally in the place she thrived: the true center of attention, the specimen in the lab, the cause for concern. It felt good to let the words balloon in my mouth. Munchausen. Factitious. But as I kept looking at her those words shrunk and seemed silly. Nothing could define Sara.

"I missed you so much, but what you said hurt so much too. Maybe now you'll see that it really is my body wasting away, not some mental issue. Just look at the tests, there's been blood in my urine too, some sort of infection."

Why had I been so scared all this time? So hesitant to take her completely for myself? She looked so tiny in bed. Beautiful. Helpless. Sara was nothing without me to validate her bizarre fragility. I pushed my head down to her chest and held her sides with my arms. I breathed her in, her rose-musk scent not as strong as I remembered, but still, it smelled like home. The nurse cleared her throat. "Madam, if you don't mind, she just has had some sedatives, she needs to rest."

"Go," Sara said, "we will talk later. Let Rahil tell you all about it." She closed her eyes rather dramatically.

Rahil and I walked to the hospital canteen in silence. At first Rahil charged ahead, expecting me to catch up. But I slowed him down, taking tiny, considered steps. It's fascinating how you can get anyone to do anything by simply disrupting the most basic expectation he has of you. In seconds his pace matched mine. The silence was starting to add up, but I wouldn't let him win. After we had cups of juice in our hands, we found a corner table and sat down. Rahil combed his fingers through his shiny hair. He had three-day stubble. The urge to feel his tongue in my mouth surprised me.

He broke first: "Mira, I am sorry. Look, you brought up all this stuff—that fight—I mean, this is stuff I've gone through with her before, it's not like you came in and brought it to my notice, but listen." He reached for my hand. "Hey, hey, listen, you came in and you changed something, we all know that. But you have to understand, Sara is not like the rest of us, you can't define her, you can't just propose therapy for her, she doesn't work like that."

"She is a human being, Rahil, and some things can be defined. I know what she has. She has Munchausen, and you know it. In fact, I think you have it too, by proxy that is. You love this. You love taking her to doctors and hospitals and taking care of her sickly body."

It felt good to say it out loud. It felt good looking at a very startled Rahil. His eyes twitched. I saw him consciously trying not to overreact. He was going to take control of this. I could see him negotiating a response in his head. His voice came back in that distant, icy tone. This time it failed to hurt me. It was his coping mechanism.

"Congratulations, you read a stupid psychology textbook. Are you happy now? You're parroting the *DSM* from the American Psychiatric Association."

"You don't want to hear the truth, do you? You don't want to accept that—whatever you call it. I am the only one who can accept it for what it is. And I am the only one you both need."

Rahil looked like he had been stunned by a slap.

I was amazed my voice hadn't broken and tears hadn't flooded my face. A moment went by, and Rahil was back to his malleable self—the one that I had needed so desperately over the last few months. The friend who had pushed me to find love in ways I had never thought possible. The man who had allowed me to love his wife. People around us were looking. One bald man, eating his lunch idly, paused to stare blatantly.

I allowed a small grin to form. My new confidence had rewarded me with the Rahil I wanted. The Rahil I needed. I had to make him feel validated while remaining under my control. "Look, I know you didn't *do* anything, you weren't making her sick. I saw the way you looked at her. I was running myself crazy with the idea that you were probably both feeding each other with this sickness."

Rahil held my hand. "Mira, I would never do anything to hurt Sara, or you." He was looking into my eyes apologetically. "We love you."

"Then give me the keys to your house right now."

Rahil looked blankly at me, and my eyes blinked rapidly in surprise at my own words. He hadn't expected that. He had expected needy Mira. Mira who would take any scrap of affection and cradle it for days.

"The house has always been yours, Mira," Rahil said, trying to shrug.

I swirled my tongue in irritation. Whose house was it these last few months? But I couldn't react with rage.

I was controlled; I knew what I was doing. I was getting what I wanted. There was no time to have shame or second thoughts about it. Rahil broke my silence again, mostly because he had no choice. My resolve was too strong.

"It's yours, I want nothing more."

I didn't say anything. He took a deep breath, exhaled slowly.

"Mira, I need you to be okay with this. We're caught up in a fucking mad situation, but we love you, Sara loves you, and I'll be honest. I need you the most." He paused. "I am taking her home today—our home."

He fiddled in his pocket and brought out the metal key attached to a key chain shaped like an apple. He pushed his hand forward and let it dangle between us.

Like a child being coaxed by candy, I let my stringent resolve weaken just a little. "Okay," I mumbled, taking the key, hating myself, loving this moment.

We finished off our juice as he continued to tell me about life over the last two months. Sara had pushed him away, spending hours at home, not wanting to go on their evening walks. He worked harder, won a major promotion. He'd wanted to call me, he said, but Sara was not ready. They needed time to examine what they meant to each other. But then one day Sara had started opening up to Rahil, asking him if he missed me.

"It was only a matter of time. Sara knew how much you meant to me, to the both of us."

By the time we were done we had decided that I'd go home to pack some things and then leave for Sara and Rahil's house. I would stay there and wait for them to come home that evening. I told Rahil that the blood in her urine was probably from her cutting herself and adding it to her samples. He shrugged his shoulders dismissively. "You've been researching the disease, I get it, but I am years ahead of you, Mir. She has her phases, and you coming home is going to make things better, I promise."

The tiny cells in my brain that had managed to still hold fragments of sanity started to buzz. I was dizzy. For seconds I was even sane. With sanity came self-righteousness. With sanity came rationality. This was messed up. This was stupid. This situation made no sense. But it all faded in the shimmer of a second. The world was still and my heart spilled out of my chest.

An excited teenager who'd just had her first kiss—this is what I felt like. Hurrying away from the hospital, manically packing some things from my house, and, finally, swinging open the door of their home, our home. Home.

Their bed was made, but I made it again. My love went into dusting the TV table even though it was spotless. My dizzying excitement went into cutting up fruits from their fridge and decorating a platter with them. An hour later, after chamomile tea from a blue cup, I sat on their sofa imagining all the conversations we'd have, all the love we'd share in our twisted new family. Only after all this did I remember what had happened in school that afternoon. I checked my email. I was not surprised to see a message from Mr. Khan, subject line: *URGENT*. It didn't matter. I had Sara and Rahil coming home to me. Nothing could shake me. I clicked on the email, scanning it quickly.

My gut zigzagged through my body, the feeling of shame and disappointment swirling at the bottom of my stomach, getting faster, thicker, until the entire lower half of my body cramped. I stared at the email, read it again. Finally, I tapped out my reply and quickly shut the laptop, going to the kitchen and starting very slowly, very pleasurably, to make a pot of khichadi with three different lentils. I added carrots, spinach, onions, and tomatoes. I substituted quinoa instead of rice. They knocked on the door around seven. Rahil had his arm around Sara. She wore a pair of baggy jeans and a white turtleneck. They both came toward me, their arms wrapped around me. I melted into them.

At dinner we didn't discuss the hospital or the tests. I would do anything to avoid talking to Sara about Sara. I told them all about my job, and Sara was only too happy to listen, her head tilting sympathetically with every inflection in my voice.

"There's always a risk when you teach outside the lines, I know Mr. Khan had warned me about this, and Samina, she had so much potential, she just took it too far."

If there was a rock of guilt in my throat, I didn't feel it. The monster had taken over; I could make amends only after I was sure I was going to be in Sara and Rahil's life forever.

Rahil listened too, but not as actively, intent on the bowl of quinoa khichadi. He was the first to say something, though.

"You're going to get fired, you know that, right? You're lucky you aren't in America, the parents would have sued you *and* the school."

Sara elbowed him so hard his spoon fell onto the table. "She may well be fired, but what that girl did was wonderful, she facilitated something needed. Everybody in their little bubbles of school and life and boring shit, now there's a girl with real soul trying to burst through life and cut through all our stupid hypocrisies."

I shook my head. "What matters is small change, not going all the way crazy radical—then we just get shut down."

"No, Mira, you should be up front with the school. After all, you can't be held responsible for her actions, although I'm inclined to say you should defend them."

"What, be the official commie radical teacher of the Seeds school?"

Rahil burst out laughing, but no one followed him in that response.

"I will never teach again."

I couldn't admit to them that I had encouraged Samina to do something that would at the very least expel her temporarily. So I let them feel sorry for me and my convictions.

Sara sighed into her bowl. She had eaten half the serving and I knew she wouldn't finish it. She looked up again and grinned.

"Figure it out tomorrow, and don't worry, life has too many opportunities, this is nothing."

I looked up at Sara's hair muddled in a bun, shiny ends poking out toward the ceiling. What opportunities did she mean? The only opportunity I wanted was to be with them. Held together by the everyday—me, Sara,

Rahil—as natural as sunlight beaming into the bedroom window in the morning.

In the middle of the night, I left the guest room and woke Rahil and Sara up. My urge to get everything straight had given me the confidence to risk everything. It was going to have to be a straight-up demand or nothing at all. Rahil patted the middle of the bed, Sara sleepily ushered me to the spot with her arm.

"I am always going to be the third wheel," I said as I squeezed in between them. I felt the resolve of the monster fade. But wasn't vulnerability also a tool to get what you needed? I continued: "And what we're doing, it's mostly going to be a secret. You have each other, but I don't have that security. I don't even have the words to say what the two of you mean to me."

Sara held my hand. "Mira, the secrets are out, let's not try to explain it. There is no such thing as security; we're here now, feel us."

Rahil pulled my cheek to him, pressed his lips to mine. But only for seconds, then he patted the pillow, indicating it was time to sleep again. "You'll have to switch bedrooms early in the morning before Kamala comes in," Rahil said, his voice gentle but firm.

A rage erupted in my throat. But the monster told me not to roar: *Take it one step at a time, Mira.*

After which we, three peas in a pod, slept soundlessly.

XX

Mr. Khan's face was pulled tight. His eyes were sad and his hands tapped uncontrollably on the table. He asked me to sit. He squirted sanitizer on his hands, looked around awkwardly, and then handed me the bottle.

"It's my fault," he stated quietly. "The day you walked in, I knew you'd be trouble. I swear on my beating liberal heart, Mira, I wanted trouble, I wanted risk. But, lady, no one, and I am sure of it, not even you, knew it would end up like this."

I squirted a bit of the sanitizer in my hands and rubbed them together sympathetically. "I'll spare you any excuses, Mr. Khan, I know your position, and I sympathize with it. I sympathize with a world that's not ready for a few shifts. But that's not to say what happened with Samina was truly appropriate, or that a radical action by itself means anything in terms of being the renegade, I mean..."

"That's a philosophical discussion we should have when you are not a teacher, and hopefully when I am no longer leading the chain of this monkey house. Look, her parents are flipping mad, but that's the least of it, because, well, there is only so much anger they can have toward the school when it was Samina, all of seventeen, who did it herself. But I have other parents, shocked, prepared to go to the press, prepared to ask for refunds, prepared to create a revolution of sorts at the gates, and, yes, I see the irony there."

"What do I need to do, apart from taking my things and leaving the school premises for good?"

Mr. Khan sighed. "You need to take full responsibility, you need to write an email to all the parents discussing how this even came about. Make it clear you are stepping down as a teacher from Seven Seeds with your greatest of apologies. The rest I suspect will die out—after all, parents don't have the bandwidth to deal with changing schools and following up with all their anger. They have jobs to go back to."

"It'll be done."

"I am sad to let you go. I am angered you let it get this far—you were good for them." He sighed again. "All your things are with me. Thought I'd spare you the horror of stepping into the staff room again. Mira, consider becoming a writer, or a filmmaker, or something like that, where you can get away with this kind of thing, eh?"

It was the first smile he cracked and I returned it.

"We'll pay your salary for this month and release your pension fund. Oh, and, Mira." He reached into his pocket and passed me a piece of paper. "My personal email, keep in touch."

He looked back to the hand sanitizer and gave it another squirt. I left the room with my things.

At the house, Sara had placed sliced apples and peanut butter on the table. She violently nodded and told me she'd help me write the email to the parents. "Listen, don't worry about money or salaries, Rahil's new promotion can support a family of four."

I started to cry. My life had come to this. I didn't need money; I had enough saved and had plenty from Ketan's life insurance. But the fact that Sara had offered to support me like a lover, like a child, like an I'm not sure what, made me feel like less of a kept woman. This kind of bliss must only be temporary, I knew, bliss with nothing else to compare it to. Could bliss last forever after you had enough pain from the past to provide a lifetime of context?

Sara walked me over to the bedroom. We spent the afternoon hours in bed, sucking, loving, kissing, stroking, hurting, and laughing. Sara's mouth had not been freshly chewed on. It was really all becoming okay again. We had finally figured it out. Her wetness stayed on my fingers, her scent on my chest. When Rahil came back we were a family again. He kissed both of us, separately, authoritatively. Someone needed to be authoritative with it, because with authority came the illusion of normalcy.

But Rahil was inconsistent. He still didn't know what he wanted. As soon as he walked in the door I felt like the outsider, the woman whom he was indulging in order to save Sara. I knew this because he'd pick up books around the house and start reading the backs of them when he was caught alone with me. He'd go back to talking with me soon enough, but there were always these pauses: looking at his phone, book browsing, endless shiftless-ness. Like he was talking himself into this reality.

The silverware clinked, Rahil told us about his day, his new project bringing in clients from Singapore and Dubai. Then he discussed the culture of the Japanese sal-aryman. A random buffer topic, I thought, to sooth him into thinking this was a temporary dinner party.

"I told Kamala you had a bad marriage and just got divorced, and that you will be here for a long time—that shut her up for now," Sara said, breaking the lethargic tone Rahil had set.

From now on, I had to wake up at 5:30 every morning to get out of bed and run into the guest room so Kamala would just think a weird cousin was in town. A guest for an extended period of time. I had made my peace with it. It was our secret game. Kamala had treated me with sac-charine smiles so far. But every morning, she looked like she was about to pounce on me with a direct question.

"Mira." Sara's voice had changed tone. It was formal, it was assured. "I've been doing some reading and think-ing. There is so much I want to say to you, and we have many days ahead of us."

"So you think your health will hold up now, for a while at least?" As soon as the words came out I realized I was scared of a happy, healthy Sara. What would Sara sans illness mean to Rahil and me?

"Quite the opposite. I think she's had quite the revo-lution in her head, haven't you, Sara?" Rahil said as he looked up at me for a brief moment.

"Maybe," she said as she scooped one last spoonful out of her bowl and raised it to her mouth.

I was about to ask her what this new revolution was about, but Rahil's phone rang. He picked it up and walked toward the guest room.

Sara stood up. "Must be work."

She took her empty bowl into the kitchen. I sat in silence, staring at the cinnamon stick I had pulled out of the daal and placed on the corner of my plate.

Dear Parent,

I write this with a heavy heart. I am asking for you to read my letter, although I understand some of you might be too angry to have the patience to hear me out.

I don't have excuses, but I do have intent. I never planned to be a teacher, but when I was twenty-nine a personal crisis led me to books. They opened up my world so much that I had to find a place to share what I had learned. For me that place was teaching. I'll concede that my teaching had a bent, a leftist sway as some of you might call it. For those more critical, you may even call it radical.

The incident that happened this week is completely my fault. I take 100 percent accountability for letting a minor read a book and then demonstrate her understanding of it without the proper guidance.

I hope you will one day see that what Samina did was not vulgar but, at the worst, misguided and inappropriate for the situation she was in.

I, as an adult, should have known what she was going to do and talked about it with her. I hope this will not dissuade you from encouraging your children to read and learn about things that might not fit in with what we consider to be correct and normal for their academic life.

I hope you will encourage them to channel their knowledge and even offer them comments and time for discussions about their knowledge. The thing is, children interpret this world uniquely, and while we all need to have one uniform way of getting some base points across through traditional schooling, we must allow them to find their own perspective. The world quite depends on it.

All this is not to say that I am not mortified at the way I handled things.

I have resigned from my position as a teacher at Seven Seeds. This school has given your children many happy experiences and opportunities for learning; please let this one incident not taint your understanding of this school.

If you have any questions at all, please feel free to contact me. Otherwise I have left the Seven Seeds premises, effective of this afternoon at noon.

I wish you and your family all the very best.

Sincerely,
Mira Krishna

We sent off the email together, all our fingers on the send button. It was done. I found myself in the middle of their bed again that night. Rahil whispered, "We'll buy a bigger bed tomorrow." And we drowned the rustling sheets in laughter.

My days were so much longer with no job, but still, there was never enough time. We draped ourselves in blankets, we channel surfed TV. But mostly Sara told me about the path to God. The illusion of self was our enemy, she said. But it was also our only friend for lifetimes at a time.

"There are four paths to God: one is through meditation, then there is action, there is the path of knowledge, and finally the path of devotion.

"Sometimes we use all four paths, but the end is the same, it is God, it is light. I was confused, Mira, I thought I was on the path of devotion, where I had devoted my soul to light, wasting away the body, but it was the wrong way. I didn't stop to recognize that the body was also my friend. And without it I had no vehicle to get anywhere. Rahil gave me the freedom to live my paths the way I wanted, but you, Mira, you allowed me to understand what path I need to take."

"What path is that?" I asked, trying not to show how elated I was upon hearing my role, my value in her life, defined.

"The path of action. I am still figuring it out, but I have some ideas. When it's time, you will be the one to understand it the most."

I let Sara shroud her new epiphany in the mystery and confusion it deserved. She was weak and complained of knee pain, but she had more energy than I ever remembered. She traipsed through the house, making tea, cutting fruit, feeding me bits of cut vegetables. We looked up recipes on the internet: Indonesian coconut curry and homemade cacao-almond ice cream. We made food from her childhood: raisin pulao tempered with ghee-fried cardamom and cinnamon sticks. We made hearty daal and bright salads; we painted our bedroom light blue. And in the evenings we huddled watching movies.

One Sunday we walked to breakfast without a particular destination, Sara's hand firmly in mine as Rahil led us. We walked on residential lanes, moving farther away from our neighborhood, until middle class blurred into very upper middle class, where bungalows with towering gates were laced with purple bougainvillea vines. We found a quaint little café that was run out of a home. We ordered toast, coffee, and fruit bowls. Sara ate everything on her plate. I didn't say anything, but Rahil looked at her and smiled as if she were a child who had eaten all her vegetables.

Afterward we walked again until we reached the park. The park I used to go to every weekend. The one that had led us to each other. But none of us said anything. My heart became heavy with excitement as we passed by the same bench where I had first seen Sara. I could have sworn she paused for a millisecond. She was about to say something. My body had mimicked her pause, waiting for her to remember with me. Instead she looked to the other side, pointing her finger toward the banyan trees. "Let's go there," she said.

We both followed in silence.

Are you wondering about Rahil and I? It's simple, or at least it became simple. Sara herself pushed the two of us to the guest room one night. "Sometimes you need to find each other with the privacy that being a couple offers. Mira, don't feel shy, we are all too special to feel awkward."

There was no awkwardness when she said these words. There was only the unheard sigh of internal relief. She had just articulated something that was supposed to have been understood a long time ago. Something that should have been understood the very first day we met. We were here to form a different kind of family, one not too many people would want to understand, but one, of course, they would like to know about.

Sara sat back on the sofa and opened a book. She raised her head, her chin nudged us. "Go on, it's okay."

And Rahil took the lead, holding my hand, taking me to the bedroom, closing the door. Closing the door on Sara.

"Look, we don't have to have sex just because she has forced us into the room."

And of course we laughed. We laughed so hard, Sara yelled from the other room to shut up. We kissed, we cuddled, we frolicked in the room in which Sara had given us permission to. When we came out later, Sara was in the kitchen boiling water for tea.

I remember a friend I had in college who studied abroad in San Francisco. She wrote to me about a three-some who lived together and also slept with other people individually. I had laughed at those emails, replied, *Oh, that'll never happen openly in India, what an idea, though.*

I was so naive then, I thought it was the silliest thing I'd ever heard. Later, when I was with Ketan, I told him about it. He said that humans weren't meant to be monogamous, or at the very least should be able to find love and bonds outside their most socially sanctioned intimate ones. I had felt threatened and immediately started crying. He had gathered me in his arms and said something that immediately relieved me. "That's just in theory, Mir-Mir. The truth is I love you and can't see any kind of life without you. Ever."

I hadn't argued further with Ketan. His words were enough because I knew Ketan wouldn't go anywhere. Rahil, though—he had forced me to demand what I wanted. Rahil was an open invitation. My very presence demanded that he articulate through his eyes, his body, and his words: *I love you Mira, I can't live without you.*

I told Sara this story on the couch one afternoon. "Thing is, I want to feel that one love sometimes, that safety of Ketan, but that's just me going back to something that is predictable and pleasurably thick in my memory. We always want to go back to a time we know for sure nothing bad happened. Now, every time I look at you, I think you'll be ill again, die on us."

Sara gave a full-throated giggle. "I won't die, I'll live, and you'll be surprised. I promise you that."

Her words made me happy. Her words made me worried.

Sara's parents called in the mornings, something I had never been privy to before in my past life with them. Rahil had told me that when she talked to her parents her voice was choked and stifled. But what I witnessed was different. Sara was assured, confident, articulate. Lately her parents had been calling and asking her to come visit them—a request Sara always half committed to with vague answers. Instead she redirected with spiritual advice. *Fear is a thought and only a thought.* She said it to her mother at some point in every conversation. What would my mother have said if I told her her sadness was a thought and only a thought?

I asked Sara this one afternoon. Now I truly sought knowledge from Sara. Hers was no longer a mind that I sympathized with and indulged. These days there was a glow in her voice that seemed to hold the answers to all the questions my books had asked me. We took to bantering. But she almost always won with her tight, confident sentences.

"But, Sara, isn't it pointless to say sadness, fear, anything for that matter, is just a thought? The reality is that people have to deal with it. After all, if grief was just a thought, then I could have talked myself out of feeling it."

"And that's the point, Mira. It's the awareness you require. The awareness that you can realize it's just a thought. Everything is harnessed by the way you choose to see the world. Until we are ready to see the power of our mind, thoughts won't just be thoughts. They will be terrible things to deal with."

The profoundness of what she said was magnified by her confident articulation. It was startling. For so long, Sara had felt like an unstable element. Before pressing her or challenging her in any way, I'd always stopped to calculate her fragility, but that no longer felt necessary.

I held her wrist and fiddled with her wooden bangle. If something *had* truly changed in her, then she would be ready for my honest questions too. Something we had never acknowledged together.

"Then you'd agree that much of the illness you have experienced was just a thought. A mental illness, or what some might label as factitious disorder."

I braced for her reaction. But her wrist relaxed in my palm. "Yes. It was just a thought, a reality I created. I just wasn't aware of how powerful my mind was. I just wasn't aware of how much safety I required as an adult. So I channeled it into illness. Perhaps I still do, Mira, but I see now that I can make any reality I want."

I wasn't sure what to say. She looked at me knowingly.

"Don't be surprised, everyone can change in mighty ways. But don't look at me in such awe, Mira, your answers must come from you."

A rush of insecurity twisted my insides. She could already see that her role in my life had changed so dramatically. And yet, I could see that this very evolution was the reason I loved her. These answers had always been inside of her waiting to tumble out. It's why I'd fallen in love with her the very first time I saw her. She had strength buried under her fragile skin. It made sense. When you meet someone you are immediately attracted to, it's actually the hidden potential that draws you. It's just that not everyone gets to see that potential.

Sara stroked my cheek with her fingers and guided my head to her lap. Rahil woke me up after some time. Sara was no longer on the couch. I could hear the kettle whining from the kitchen.

I hadn't visited Appa since I'd left school. I was scared to tell him I was no longer a teacher. I could feel the bitter disappointment that would plague him once he heard of it. But I couldn't put him off any longer—Appa knew something was wrong. A fatherly sense, as he called it on the phone. I made up the perfect story: I was back with my boyfriend, his name was Rahil, and could I bring him over for dinner? Appa's voice went a note higher, confused but steady in his assurances.

Sara clapped her hands together when she heard. "I'll be Rahil's sister, who lives with him. We can make up a nice backstory, it will be kinder this way, for your father."

I was the only one who saw Rahil flinch. I caught that microsecond, with time stopped, and I counted the number of new lines that popped on his face in worry. And then, like the perfect husband, his face relaxed into sweet acceptance. A mellow, friendly encouragement that was meant just for Sara.

I knew Sara was right, it was the most honest I could get with Appa. Although he had found it in himself to be truthful about my mother, how many other memories and secrets was he still holding back? Surely there were many, enough to keep him company in the nights and in the long mornings he had to himself. We were each entitled to our own stories, our own memories, and how we made them.

I called Appa back to tell him it would be me, Rahil, and his sister Sara for dinner.

"Sara," Appa said. "I've always loved the simplicity of that name."

On Saturday, Appa welcomed us with exuberance. Perhaps it was the realized hope even the most feminist of fathers still holds on to: that his daughter will find a man to love her, to take care of her.

He wore brown tailored pants and a button-down off-white shirt. He ushered us into the living room, where the coffee table was laden with namkeens and chili-powder-freckled potato chips. He had glasses of Thums Up poured out with small ice cubes floating on the top, just beginning to melt.

"Ah, so, Rahil, I finally meet you, but let me get to know your beautiful sister first."

Sara blushed, pulled her hair back, and charmed the pants off my father. She said she had recently divorced and had moved from Delhi to take a break for a year and live with her brother. The ease of her lies made me uncomfortable, only because Appa believed them. Why wouldn't he, after all? Appa's earnest interest in everything Sara was saying forced envy to swell in my chest. She asked him questions about his life, particularly about his work with the residential committee. Sara said she had heard he was a history buff and asked him to share a list of books with her, books that he thought she ought to read.

Rahil sat on the side, half nervous, but half, I suspect, at peace. Sara had an uncanny ability to take control of a situation, to be an accessible enigma, and everybody—even my father—wants to be as near as possible to an accessible enigma.

Suitably impressed with Rahil's career credentials, Appa asked him questions about his head of sales position. And he asked about Rahil's parents.

"My grandfather was from Agra, my mother from Delhi," Rahil said, and then proceeded to give Appa a quick summary of his background.

"Ah, so your grandfather was a spice trader. Agra, what a special spot in this country!" Appa was about to give us a historical anecdote, I could feel it. He cleared his throat. "The rumor is that Shah Jahān died in Musamman Burj. It was a tower, and from the balcony you could see the Taj Mahal."

Sara enthused, "You're a walking encyclopedia."

"Oh, not me—Mira used to be one. She has gotten dusty in the last few months, those kids at school distracting her with silly music and bands, eh, Mira?"

The room ran into silence. Rahil and Sara looked at me expectantly. "Actually, I've been meaning to tell you, Appa, I resigned from my job at Seven Seeds."

He didn't say anything; his forehead was a map of lines, frozen, waiting for me to go on.

"I just needed a change, that's all, don't worry. I might apply to some schools next month again."

Appa shrugged his shoulders. He smiled at me, and his smile held me in place. "Well, Mir-Mir, whatever makes you happy."

In this moment, I almost wanted to tell him the truth: that I hadn't resigned, that things had happened. I know he would have been proud that I had pushed the students to think, and think critically. But of course, that wasn't really the truth either. And my own interest in pushing, in fighting for critical thinking, was leaving me. The grief I had felt for Ketan, it was leaving me too. All I wanted was Sara, Sara and Rahil and our house.

We sat to dinner; Appa had asked the cook to make fresh appams and vegetable stew. There was also a host of other dishes: chickpea curry, sprout salad, onion raita, and capsicums stuffed with spiced basmati rice.

"Mira might have told you; I am quite a strict vegetarian," Appa said. "If you see how the animals are treated today, you'll know half the fear and pain in this world is consumed and rebirthed."

Sara's eyes lit up again. She was quite the Christmas tree with Appa. "You know, you are right, Uncle, absolutely, we've all become unthinking robots. No wonder we have become apathetic to blood, and war, and whatever else is thrown our way in those newspapers. When we fill our stomachs with the deaths of thousands, what else do you expect from us? I have been thinking about going vegetarian myself."

Appa put a piece of his appam down in surprise. "Yes, exactly my thoughts."

I rolled my eyes. The urge to needle was fierce. "Well, if it's about violence to animals, you ought to give up dairy, it's terrifically cruel. And might I add the beef industry in India relies on the dairy industry, all those milked-out cows go right to the slaughterhouse."

Samina had pumped me with this information. She had tried to go vegan, but her parents hated the idea. I already knew Sara would say she didn't use milk anymore, but she did eat meat. And Appa had yogurt at every meal, along with plenty of milk in his coffee. I liked the conflict I had created even though I had no interest in examining my own food choices. Appa cleared his throat. I sensed his answer would be vague even before he said anything.

"Ah, well, Mira, one grand expulsion of everything violent in this world would render us insignificant to the universe. After all, we all have spiritual leaps to make. Or scientific leaps, if that makes you happier to say it that way." Appa clasped his hands in uncertainty. "Well, as Mahatma Gandhi once admitted, I too am a creature of habit, but I appreciate the fact that you are thinking about these things, Mira. I've always said fear and food are linked."

"A habit is just a thought," I said, and winked at Sara.

I felt stupid as soon as I said it. Appa and Sara were on the same page. Sara just giggled in response: a rising sharp laugh that was directed at Appa. He was both flattered and weary at the same time, I could sense it. But wasn't that what we all were when it came to Sara?

Rahil had been nodding along to everything everyone said, as if he had entered our minds, agreeing with each opinion and phrase at its authentic source. Who was Rahil? Was he spineless or just accepting? Neither. He was the lifeboat that kept us all afloat as we created crashing walls of water. He was Sara. He was me. And tonight he was Appa too.

By the time we had been served two gulab jamuns in glass bowls for dessert, Sara had managed to rope Appa into a conversation about Sufism. Appa, of course, had to get his bit in, and he went right into a story, looking at Rahil, Sara, and me for equal amounts of time as he spoke:

"Now, many countries in the Middle East want to claim Rumi as their national poet, hah! But these countries didn't even exist in Rumi's time. Anyway, what many people don't talk of is Rumi's own inspiration. Rumi's friend, or master, or what some may like to call his greatest influence, was Shams Tabrizi. Rumi met him in his thirties. Their relationship was complex, intense; it was the reason that Rumi became a true mystic, if you ask me. But then Shams was killed, some say by Rumi's jealous disciples. Rumi wrote thousands of poems in grief, love, and pure ecstasy for Shams. That was his golden work, the *Diwan-e Shams-e Tabrizi*. You know what I say? When I look back at my life, I'd say these are the only kind of relationships, or friendships, worth having. Ones that change who you fundamentally are, ones that push you to be a waltzing, wandering, mystical fool."

We laughed. I felt like a waltzing, wandering, mystical fool.

My heart filled my chest with its thudding. Whether Appa sensed anything or not, his anecdotes and depth of knowledge in something that wasn't politics or history surprised me. I barely knew Appa at all. And yet, I knew him well enough. Rahil had managed to ask him about his fascination with the World Wars. Appa started to respond but his voice faded. I couldn't hear anything beyond a calm buzz. A happy Sara, an engaged Rahil, and a very excited Appa in a circle of conversation, their voices a murmur. I could have watched them all night.

XXI

How
Did the rose
Ever open its heart

And give to this world
All its
Beauty?

It felt the encouragement of light
Against its
Being,

Otherwise,
We all remain

Too

Frightened.

—Hafiz

I hadn't looked for a new job. I was occupied by life, truly I was. I didn't need to convince anyone. I was breathing occupation: I read poems for Sara in the morning; we watched trash TV in the afternoon; we discussed work and politics with Rahil on Saturday; and we took long drives out of the city on Sunday. Drives where buildings quickly dropped in size, became the same height, and the coffee thicker with chicory. We were insular, we were pristine, we were fucking lovely.

Some Sunday afternoons, when Sara slept, Rahil came to me. We found the time to inhale our caresses and exhale them right back. Our sex was calmer now, easier, and more loving. And Sara, with her internal body clock and her heightened soul, always awoke after we were done. She always remembered the tea, the dried chamomile blooming in the heat of the water. There were times, before dinner, when Rahil would go into Sara's room and casually shut the door. I didn't know if they had sex—if they did they were awfully quiet. Suddenly alone, I'd pick up my laptop and focus on trying to feel casual about it.

At first I was troubled by my lack of memory of what I used to be. After Ketan. Before Ketan. I was troubled by the fact that I'd forgotten the names of the philosophers who used to be on the tip of my tongue. I couldn't remember which famous philosopher had supported the Nazis, although I was certain his name started with *H*. I couldn't remember if Plato came before Aristotle. I feared loss at a cellular level. I was aghast that I didn't even feel the need to google these simple answers. But my memory was all right. I knew this because I could remember things from years before, but they were all smells, visions, and expressions. I could no longer recall inferences, contextual references, or pedagogy. Knowledge was no longer my anchor. Instead it was the simplicity of nothingness. It was the sturdy calm sips of tea I took. My reliance on books had evaporated when I lost them, but the knowledge had still been there, a safety belt that had explained my world. Now that no longer mattered either.

Sara's sickness had been lifted. She refused to do too much outside, insisting she needed her rest. But she was rarely tucked away in bed for more than an hour in the daytime. She meditated now, the room closed, the trail of music wandering cautiously out to the living room, where I sat surfing the internet or reading tweets from people whom I used to know. She was detangling her thoughts and making new ones. It urged me to deconstruct my own thoughts too.

When I was in bed with Rahil, though, I felt the empty beauty of not thinking at all. The understanding that my peace came from something so very simple was equal parts humbling and infuriating.

I woke up, sweat sticky on my palms, after one of my nights spent with Rahil. I had a dream: Samina locked in a room. She had not eaten as a result of a punishment her parents had given her. In the dream, I understood that Samina's parents had asked me for a suitable punishment for their daughter and it was I who had recommended starving her. She looked up from her bed, eyes pleading with me.

I shot up straight in bed, and just as quickly Rahil's arms were around me, his prompt support feeling so authentic, like something he'd do for Sara.

"I had a dream about Samina, it's all my fault," I mumbled without thinking. But Rahil didn't probe. He held me for another ten minutes. Right before I fell off to sleep his words appeared thick and warm in my ears: "I know, I know."

In the morning, nothing was discussed. I didn't know what Rahil knew or thought he knew. Regardless, one thing was clear: Rahil was born to take responsibility of someone. To inherit ownership of whatever card life decided to deal.

I was making sure I was a part of his hand.

Ten days away from flying to her parents' home, Sara said, "Once I am in that house, they will track my every move, but when I am here with Rahil, it's almost like I don't exist to them."

"Out of sight, out of mind," Rahil said drily.

"Well, more like they use whatever is around them to project their fears, maybe it's on their house help, Shanta. She lives full-time with them, poor girl."

Later, Rahil told me it was the most critical thing Sara had said about her parents in her life, or at least in front of Rahil. He sounded happy about this, but he looked unsettled too. Typical Sara effect. It was the same effect that drove me to her. Sara held truths about the world; she didn't need to apply them to herself in order to make you feel like the ignorant one.

I was nervous about her departure. It would only be for ten days, but it would be ten days of me in the house without her, without a job, waiting for Rahil. What would I do with my time? I could read again. I could visit Appa more. I could get a job. I could do a lot, but I didn't want to. I wanted the calm of my new life. I wanted not to think about anything that demanded interaction with the outside world.

That afternoon, Sara talked about Rahil with clinical precision, the kind that comes with years of observation and unconditional love.

What Sara Told Me About Rahil

When the quintessential middle-class family gives birth to a son, there is an unsaid demand. The child will be at the very least above average in school. There will be plenty of childhood memories, ones that can be passed off as mischievous at worst, like Rahil peeing on the watchman's head at age four from the terrace. These stories will vary in detail at first, but soon enough they will congeal as one story the adult son will tell his wife and pass down to his children. The son as a teenager will be studious enough and have a reliable hobby: music, cricket, movies.

He will have many friends, and the friends will be similarly disciplined. The adult son will go to college; if the family is lucky, he will finish a master's degree abroad. The ideal son comes back, finds a reliable job with steady promotions, gets married: a same-region, same-caste love marriage is most acceptable, even preferred in some urban scenes. Otherwise a modern arranged marriage is expected by the time he is twenty-seven, thirty for those who have created a blazing fire trail with their career. A child within two years, and the parents can finally sigh with relief. They have successfully brought up a straitlaced *nice Indian guy*. The one who will not be too political. The one who will latch on to anything the government does with technology and New India. The one who will read a few books here and there, but limit the amount they can move him. The one who will say, "My daughter's career comes first," but will inevitably squirm the moment she is twenty-five and single.

"The thing is, procreation is reliable, scientific, and easy, and that's the result they want for the next thirty years too. Maybe there is nothing wrong with it, but can we just say it's dreadfully boring?" Sara said to me, as she broke a wheat cracker into tiny bits.

Rahil's mother, it turned out, was a gynecologist who gave up practicing after Rahil was born. His father was a reasonably well-off businessman who had inherited from his grandfather's spice trading fortune. Now he had his own factory. Rahil had ticked off most of the boxes to become a straitlaced nice Indian guy. With self-effacing humor, he could recite his standard childhood memory of peeing on top of the watchman's head from the terrace. He was studious enough to take the exams to get into the Indian Institute of Technology but hadn't made the cut. Surprise came in the form of him wanting to study in Delhi, for a degree in business.

His parents weren't happy and only became more concerned when he fell in love with Sara. When he got his first job and moved up on luck and talent, they called it a win. After all, he had a steady job and was married.

Both Sara and Rahil were only children, but unlike Sara's, his parents weren't obsessed with his well-being. And they had no relationship with Sara; it was only Rahil who visited them once a year in Agra. Sara was inarguably a disappointment as a traditional wife so, for all practical purposes, they treated him as a bachelor son. Despite this marital failure, he maintained the strait-laced nice Indian guy image in their eyes, making good money, living life like any other successful son.

"You'd think there might be more to him, more of a story, but really he loves what he does, and it's the small things that make him happy: coming home at a predictable time, drinking a beer on a Friday night, watching movies, cuddling, reading the news, and, once in a while, socializing with his work friends. Everything about him is predictable except his love for me, and now us."

"He won't ever love me the way he loves you, and he can't love you the way I do," I whined. "We really don't talk about how odd we are—"

"That's the thing, it's normal because we simply *are* this way."

"I'm not sure any of our parents would agree with that logic."

"Mira, you think too much. You need to intellectualize it, or find a way for it to be ideal. The thing is, it is just another relationship—its ideal nature is never going to be the reality. Forget obsessing over us."

"It's hard not to," I said quietly. I was hoping she'd indulge me, say something magical that would make me feel completely and unquestionably loved. Sara's conviction in her words was only making me panic. "So you just think this is fine, we're nothing special, just our version of normal?"

Sara shook her head gently as she got up from the couch and straightened out a crinkle on her cream tunic. She looked down at me; I couldn't tell if her eyes offered pity or compassion.

"You must do more, Mira, don't you think?"

XXII

In the beginning, there was purpose to us, to Sara; now, it had become the entire point of my life. I was unemployed, I wasn't doing anything to change that, and I didn't even know what I wanted. I wanted to be here, every day, to wake up to tea, wake up to Sara and Rahil. And yet something was changing.

A week before her departure to Delhi, Sara ordered that we each have three hours of "research time" every day while Rahil was at work. Rahil obliged her because he considered it a part of her new personal revolution, her path to health. I obliged her because I'd do anything that would make Sara happy and rely on me. She spent her three hours in her bedroom. I stuck to the guest room. We were allowed to use books, the internet, and notebooks.

"I must find something to do with my life, Mira. You and Rahil, you've kicked something in me, you refused to leave me to waste away. Now you've started a fire in my head."

My first response was a need to control her. A need to stop her. I was acutely self-aware of the irony. I felt like a jealous husband who had just been told that his wife was getting another promotion and would now make more money than him.

She spun around in the living room. Sara was easy to take seriously—her movements demanded it—but her twirl just looked silly. "I feel something, I feel like I know why I used to be the way I used to be."

"What do you mean?" I asked, standing up next to her.

"The best way I can explain it is that my thoughts are my life, and my thoughts have changed into something joyous."

I stood there, a helpless child, looking at Sara, an adult woman who had found the secrets she was born with. The ones hidden behind her self-doubt and cloistered past. It meant something, only I didn't feel intelligent enough to decode it. Life here was trying so fucking hard to illustrate its truth, I could feel its force swirling around the room. So close I could breathe it. Sara looked at me, all-knowing and compassionate. "It's okay to be wherever you are right now—say it, say it with me."

"It's okay to be wherever you are right now."

We chanted it together like we were in some hokey spiritual workshop. But just when I thought we were done, she sat on the floor and kept repeating it.

"It's okay to be wherever you are right now."

It was like the beginning again. When she would sway on her bed, so ill she couldn't stand. And I would join her without question, until I felt it to be the most normal thing to do. I held her hands and joined her on the floor. I chanted in whispers. I chanted until the words became alien humming. Until I felt Sara's hands slip from mine. When I opened my eyes, she was there.

Present. Lips curved into a soft smile. Eyes bouncing with thoughts I couldn't begin to understand.

Sara became increasingly cagey in the afternoons, fiercely protective of her time alone in her room, doing God knows what. I was forced to scroll the internet. Books were no longer an idea even worth toying with; history no longer fascinated me. I watched YouTube clips, I browsed new schools' job openings—international schools that were banking on upper-middle-class anxieties, ones that would take teachers who were willing to do what the job demanded. But of course my qualifications were dependent solely on my experience at Seven Seeds and a good recommendation from Mr. Khan. I hadn't even dared to email Samina to learn what had happened to her. I could no longer value myself as a good candidate to teach.

By the time I looped this entire sequence of thought in my head, I felt thoroughly bored with the idea of a job. I considered going back to a mainstream corporate job and started to use my afternoon hours to look at traditional job platforms. But I knew I was just buying time. I was waiting to smell the chamomile wafting in the air, my signal to come outside for tea.

"So what have you been up to?" I asked Rahil. "What's new at work? I've become a dim-witted bore."

Sara was in the kitchen and I was done making issues of things, but I needed to know if Rahil was being obtuse to Sara's changes. His control in the house had worn effortlessly.

"I am excited for Sara," he said, ignoring my attempt at small talk, understanding what I was really asking. An answer like this would have riled me up even a month before. But today it calmed me. It pushed me an inch closer to thoughts Sara had been seeding in me.

I left Rahil outside and went into the kitchen, hugging Sara from behind. She turned from the pot of daal she was stirring, held my cheeks with her palms. Her smell still moved my body. "I want to tell you, Mira, you are going to be fine, Rahil is going to be fine. You're on your path and I am on mine. There is nothing to be worried about. Promise me you won't worry?"

And the insecurity slipped violently out again. Her confidence eroded my nest. I wanted to tear her hair out. I wanted her to assure me everything was going to just be the same. But I couldn't play such theatrics in the face of the calm she presented. I went back outside, where Rahil still sat.

"She's up to something."

Rahil turned to me, his voice dropped to a low whisper. "She's happy, Mira, and healthy. And it's because of you. We are lucky, to find this kind of harmony. Listen, whatever it is with her, it's because of her trip to see her parents. She always gets crazy when she has to visit."

"You're telling me her being so physically able, so bright in composure, this is normal for her?"

He snapped back faster than I thought he could. "Are you telling me you preferred her sick and wasting away?"

"Are you telling me that you haven't noticed your wife of almost a freaking decade is different?"

"Answer my question first," he said with an irritating calmness.

"It's complex. Something that seems healthy might actually be the most devastating to her right now. You aren't thinking. And yes, you might know her best, but sometimes you need a new perspective too, Rahil."

Nobody said anything; we both had our answers in the curves of our lips.

Sara increased the volume of her Sufi music, drowning out her coughing from the tempered curry leaves that must have just hit the oil.

XXIII

The moon came to me last night
With a sweet question.

She said,

"The sun has been my faithful lover
For millions of years.

Whenever I offer my body to him
Brilliant light pours from his heart.

Thousands then notice my happiness
And delight in pointing
Toward my beauty.

Hafiz,
Is it true that our destiny
Is to turn into Light
Itself?"

And I replied,

Dear moon,
Now that your love is maturing,
We need to sit together
Close like this more often

So I might instruct you
How to become
Who you
Are!

—Hafiz

The night before Sara left for Delhi we were all happy. She didn't impose her three-hour rule and Rahil came home early from work. We ate dinner together. Rice dotted with peas and cinnamon. Yellow daal with fresh coriander sprinkled on top. Cucumber slices peppered and salted. And carrots and potatoes in a mild coconut milk gravy. Sara truly had stopped eating meat after dinner with Appa. It was only Rahil and I who made chicken curry in a small pot to accompany our daal and vegetable sabji on some nights. We watched an Iranian film with subtitles. Then Rahil found a pack of old cards in our bedroom. We played rummy. We sipped Old Monk mixed with freshly brewed black tea and lemon. Rahil switched to whisky after one round of the rum. We were eating Oreos and chocolate chip cookies, a combination that was heavy in theory but felt light today.

The thoughts that went through my head in between sips and chews are what I imagine newlywed housewives think about. Ten days without her would go fast enough, I thought, and then it would be done and we'd be back to this moment. I had already planned fun things to do with Rahil while she was away. My confidant, my reliable Rahil, who absorbed my insecurities and unpredictable responses. Rahil who readily accepted my simple desires. Rahil who didn't demand the burden of my rusting intellectual barriers. We'd get on just fine, and she'd be back soon enough.

"Promise to write us emails chronicling your parents' antics?" Rahil teased, a goofy grin spreading on his face.

"Don't be rude, Rahil," she said, playfully enough. Sara had her brown hair down over her shoulders. Her hair had grown so much since I had first met her. It touched her breasts. There were split ends, but it was thick, vibrant, almost shining. She had recently decked out her wrists with multiple wooden bangles, and it seemed as if they'd always been a part of her—she even slept with them on. I had woken up to them pressing into my back the last few mornings. Every sunrise, a reminder that there was something stronger about Sara.

She sipped her rum-laced iced tea and shuffled the pack of cards. "If only you could see what I see in front of me, at this very moment. You'll see it, but later on, I promise, just remember I said this."

Rahil rolled his eyes. "Ahhhh, wise guru Sara."

Sara shook her head playfully but looked at me with intensity, like a teacher who inadvertently looks at her favorite student to shout out the answer. She expected me to understand whatever it is that she understood, not Rahil. The self-importance radiated through my body and I forgot to notice that I didn't, in fact, understand.

That night we listened to a guitarist whom Rahil had been enthralled with on YouTube. We held on to pillows, shifted our weight on the bed, and crisscrossed our legs. Our eternal slumber party. It came with the kind of sleep where you have a thousand dreams. When you wake up you can't remember them, but you're left with the feeling that you've lived multiple lifetimes through the course of the night.

The next morning was a Saturday. We helped Sara with her final packing. Phone charger, contact lens solution, earphones, and a book of poems by Hafiz in her hand baggage. Her larger suitcase was filled with freshly ironed clothes: white linens, pastel blues, ankle-length pajamas, and cotton pants. When no one was looking I pressed my face against the clothes folded in the bag. Rich rosy musk, Sara all over.

We packed a plastic box with carrot sticks, hummus, and grapes and threw it in her handbag. As we made our way to the car, I purposefully trailed behind, the slowest to board. A petulant child grousing because a parent was leaving her for a work trip.

Rahil hummed an old Hindi song. Sara sat in the front. I took my place in the middle of the back seat, watching the side of her face, making small talk. We were quiet in the car, the traffic relentless. The horns blared into the sun.

As we passed the first signboard for Suryam International Airport, decorated with pretty Rasagura fruit along its edges, I saw Rahil's left hand gently squeeze Sara's shoulder. Seconds passed, but she didn't reciprocate with so much as a glance his way. He looked to her in confusion but quickly turned his head back to the road. As we approached the airport the roads got better and the surrounding greenery more manicured.

"Don't you love how the government gives us first-world development around the airport? At least for ten kilometers we can pretend we live in Europe."

Her voice sliced the stress in the car. I laughed back in response, utterly relieved that Sara had said something inconsequential.

At the departure gate, she turned to hug us individually. She held Rahil for a long time, too long. Jealousy snaked around my body and tightened around my chest. She whispered in his ear. But then she came to me, held me, for how long I am not sure. "Everything is going to be okay. I love you."

She walked off, handing her identification card to a bored mustached security guard. We waved at her once more and she disappeared into a crowd of shuffling travelers. Rahil and I walked to the car in silence. Once I sat in the front seat, he turned toward me. "What did she tell you?"

"Huh? Nothing, just that she was happy."

"No, about the letters."

"What letters?"

"She told me there are two letters under the mattress in our bedroom, one for me and one for you, and that we should read them privately."

"What the fuck?"

I immediately called her. I was surprised when she picked up. "Yes, Mira, I'm just getting to security."

"No, what letter? Why did you write us letters? What are you up to?"

I could hear her grinning. "Uff, just read them, they are under the mattress. Gotta go now, and like I said, stop worrying."

Rahil shrugged his shoulders. "She used to write me letters when she visited her parents, but she used to send them to me. First time she has written one before she left. She is just getting wilder with age."

And that's when I realized I couldn't quite remember the last time Sara had complained of a symptom. She had been healthy for weeks, even months. And now, she was gone.

Sara's Letter to Me

Dear Mira,

At first I wanted to be poetic. But I thought I owed you something more straightforward. A marriage is another kind of relationship altogether. You know this too, because any summary you gave me of Ketan cannot hold all your stories. It can't account for the thousand things that made your relationship a living thing. It simply can't be articulated. Marriage will always remain a shared private history.

It is for this reason I ask that you never read the letter I wrote to Rahil. Not because there is any secret or fact that I have withheld here, but because there must be sanctity in what we meant to each other. Every relationship has its own story, so I ask that you never give this letter to Rahil either.

I have gone to Delhi, but I am not going to my parents' home. I'm leaving from Delhi on a bus, a carefully laid out route, with ample research and internet friends to aid with rest stops until I reach a place high above the plains. It is there where I will start to truly understand what Rumi and Hafiz meant: to find ecstasy as a wanderer, to find God in the self, to unite with ordinary in an extraordinary way.

Mira, the first thing you'll think (and Rahil will too) is that this is a little trip I've planned to find some independence. I won't lie, it started out like that at first. A little trip by myself, something so simple to do, but something I had never done.

I had fears, Mira, of anything upsetting my life. Someone leaving, dying—someone who would not be there to care for me. I was wild with fear, just wild. Yes, it made me sick, so sick that sickness became my solace. Sickness was my reassurance that something, someone, some hospital, some man, some person, would take care of me.

So yes, I thought taking a little trip would help me.

But that was the idea I had when I first met you. You gave me this unexpected courage. You let me think that there would be more. More people, more intimacy, more things for me to count on. It sounds selfish—it is—but let me go on.

But then I fell in love with you. I never stopped loving Rahil. The thing is, I loved him more thoroughly after you. More purely. Rahil was my rock, but you never appreciate a rock, it stays there waiting. The only thing that made me appreciate anything about Rahil was the feeling of fear I felt when I thought about the chance of losing him. Imagine loving someone only because you fear them dying or leaving you? Love then is only fear.

Then you came in. You were my living, breathing fear. A young woman who had lost her husband. A woman who lived by herself, who did things her way and found it perfectly ordinary.

When you see your fear living, loving, eating, breathing, fucking, you can't help but feel free.

I loved you so much. I loved your head, the weird facts you'd go on about, your ordinary ability to talk of days on that farm, the books you read, the perspective you had. You made me see the simple but potent love Rahil and I shared. It almost comforted me to see that he loved you too.

I wanted to leap, do things, be okay with living life without the fear of loss. But not before I went back to my old habits.

Once I knew I loved you, fear came back at me again. I was obsessed with the fear of losing you or, worse now, losing both you and Rahil. My body turned on me again (or as you would say, my mind did) and I needed the rush of security.

It was only after losing you for two months, the ache of having lost you at my own will, that I realized my love for you might be forever. The contradiction was this: our two-month separation was not killing me either. There was another restlessness, one to be free of fear. I had felt the edges of it, and that's only because of you.

It was only at the hospital, medicated and in bed, that I knew what I had to do, what I felt was the most important thing to do. In fact I could feel myself doing it in my sleep, I could feel myself living, alone, walking on the road, some small town, a village, anywhere, walking, doing, living without a lover, without a mother or a father, without a history of fear.

Perhaps all your Foucault, Camus, and de Beauvoir said this in many complex words. But for me it is simple. You need certain people to come in and hold a mirror to your fears. You need real (the moving, breathing, unconditional, unboxed) love to be able to see yourself and then make a choice. To walk toward freedom. And true freedom is not worrying about love and how others will perceive it as betrayal.

If anything, my going away is a testament to love, to your love. You saved me from years of being a lonely, sick woman. You saved me from dragging a man, a good-natured man, under the bus with me. For years I thought I was being the most faithful spiritualist, but now I see I was only preparing for my time, this time, as I leave, as I live.

I won't be coming back. Will I make contact? Not now, not for a few years at least, and you'll have to trust me when I say it's truly for the best. It's not for the sake of mystery or panic that I am making this decision.

It will be much better to hear from me like an old friend, a pleasant memory from the very deep past. It will be much better to hear from me when you've found your own path in life, when the rhythm of the everyday has been set, and you find yourself humming in the bathroom getting ready for your day. Then it will not be intrusive, it will not cause ache. It will just make you smile and hopefully let you remember an afternoon with me so long ago.

Mira, don't think I haven't been able to read you, understand you, know you. Not everybody's answer is taking off to start again. I see you with Rahil these days, it gives me hope. The type of steady friendship you have. The utter thrill you have with the mundane, the internet scrolling, the sofa chats. You ought to teach, you ought to write, you ought to say more things to the world. But as I write the word ought I realize the futility in it. Your ought is emerging now. I see you here, happy, and I see Rahil happy with you.

Of course you may leave the house now that I am gone. But I know this much: you won't. You might be angry, hurt, outraged. But you'll stay, and if I am right about you, you'll be happy too, not long after.

Don't try to find me, for you will not. I've done my bit: my phone will not work anymore, nor will my email. I will deal with my parents too, don't worry—neither Rahil nor you will have to deal with them ever again.

I want you to find the bliss I am carrying in my body right now. It is one with such love for the breath, for the feeling of now; it is the love that makes you fearless. And for that I will always chant your name, in the steps I take, in the food I eat, in the life I now make for myself.

Let there be only a brief moment for anger and hurt. Once it leaves you, you will begin to feel the way I do.

With all the love in my heart and head,
Sara

Epilogue

It is traditional to end a story when one of two things occurs. The first way to end it is after one has found the love of one's life. After the challenges and obstacles have ended, then so does the love story. Whether you perceive that to be happily ever after is your prerogative. The second way to end it is in tragedy. An unrequited love. A lost lover. A dead lover.

I am not ending the story because of these reasons. After all, Sara is not lost, she is only starting to find. And if she is dead, well, we won't know for sure. But her love now lives between Rahil and I. It took us months to convince ourselves that it was not a brief experiment. It took many readings of that letter to see how biblical it really was. How each sentence had been measured to reflect her rising sense of freedom. And it only took one last read, eight months into her departure, to understand that there was nothing to contest.

Nothing has changed in the house we three once used to live in. The sheets are the same colors, the kitchen as pristine and dustless (I make sure it is). We have given up drinking chamomile tea altogether. Our life had demanded coffee at some point, and now we drink it every morning. Two cups each, black, with one teaspoon of sugar.

Rahil still comes home every evening at six o'clock. We cuddle on the couch, we watch movies, we go out for walks. We stroll past that park I had given up going to since I met them. We've moved permanently to the guest room now. Sometimes we make love in Sara's bedroom. Our old bedroom.

Rahil took it worse than I did, which surprised me. I had expected to collapse, but instead I found grit and resolve. At first Rahil sulked and lowered himself into a boiling pot of depression. I didn't worry, though, because it was what Sara had predicted. His temporary descent into sadness only strengthened my conviction in Sara. I was inching closer to her truth and Rahil would undoubtedly follow. I was the calm one, the sturdy, durable one. But for me, her ache is constant and never heals. Her loss is a raw wound that stays willingly and acceptingly. For Rahil, you see scabs turning into new skin. You see new healthy tissue that has forgotten that Sara was once his, then ours, and then God's.

We played our newly invented game for months: Where Did Sara Go? We'd pick a hilly region in Himachal Pradesh and wonder what she was doing there at that very moment. We traveled with her to the northeast: Meghalaya, Nagaland, Arunachal Pradesh. We'd look up facts and obscure towns in these regions and imagine Sara living her life. She's selling tea to people in a mountain village. She is teaching history in Imphal. She has been accepted into a Buddhist monastery in Nepal. But none of our guesses gave us the satisfaction we were looking for. We stopped playing our game six months after her departure.

Appa has never asked me to marry Rahil. He is happy I live with him. He visits on the weekends. We go to Appa's all the time, and he quizzes us on pop culture and historical facts every chance he gets. Rahil has started to read more to keep up with him, while I have lost regard for any new learning. Sara had put an end to it. She had spent years accumulating the profound truths I thought only came from books. And then she put it to use. My truth was simple, it had always been. It took the loss of Sara to embrace it.

We haven't heard from Sara in three years and we've learned to live differently without her. She, in the end, was right. I was not a renegade; I was just a reader. I wasn't looking for new answers; I just wanted to find one that was comfortable enough. I have chosen my freedom within the walls of this home. Women before me wrote about these confines and made a strong case to move out of them. But here I am, and what comforts me is the fact that no man was responsible for bringing me here. It was Sara.

There is one person who is still enthralled by my mind. Samina, an adult now, at least legally. She hasn't moved out of her parents' home, but she did have the guts to email me two months after Sara left. I am her silent advocate, her cheerleader. We've been corresponding a couple times every week. She updates me on a life so different from mine: protest rallies, her academic papers, vegan outreaches, fights with the parents, and even her first sexual experiences. I respond with half-remembered quotes from those men and woman who kept me alive after Ketan. But I notice my replies have slowly shrugged off their density. Maybe it's because I know that Samina just wants my approval and support.

She'll do well for herself, move the world in her own unique way. In ways I had hoped I could. I cheerlead a shadow of myself, but my freedom remains in this house. One day soon I know I'll end up inviting her to our home for a meal.

There are levels of awareness, and each level requires a different set of coping methods. My mother had no access to alternatives. And that's okay. My father found more than her, and that's okay. I am here now, so happy at home, so thrilled with the morning coffee, with a morning kiss from Rahil. I am happy watching an old Hindi movie in the afternoon and dusting the TV and cutlery right before he comes home. I like the rhythm of folding laundry; I like teaching Manju our cook, new recipes and talking to her about her children as she washes our negligible amount of dishes every day.

We socialize too, and Rahil has moved up in his career. We've spaced out the public story we give everyone. He and Sara had divorced, and then he had quickly remarried.

In the beginning, Kamala told people in the neighborhood that I had seduced Rahil and had made Sara run away back to her parents. But no neighbor had the courage to ever ask us. We told people it was a quick court marriage. No one batted an eyelid; when you live in busy towns you can get away with such tales. Now we sit with his new colleagues on some Saturdays, interchanging houses for dinner and drinks. We go to the occasional play and watch bands at nightclubs as we sip whisky on the rocks. We talk about movie stars and enjoy making long lists for groceries. We make love fiercely, slowly, cautiously, unabashedly. We've made love in every way with every mood.

Last year the media was abuzz: Chile had managed to re-create soil conditions for Rasagura to grow. And now that the chemistry was out, they had tried it in Mexico too with decent (but low-yield) results. Our town bowed its head to science, and grandmothers were told to stop perpetuating magic tales to their grandchildren. Nothing is impossible in this world, nothing. I imagine Sara laughing at the authority of science. Was it the language of chemistry that made Rasaguras possible in Chile? Aren't things always and continuously possible, even when we lack a language to explain it?

There is a picture of the three of us in our bedroom. Sara in a white shirt, smiling between us. Her shoulder-length hair hitting my shoulder and Rahil's head curved and nestled on top of her head. We don't talk about the picture, but we both know it will always be there. We catch each other standing by it, in the early mornings or late at night. We pretend to be involved with something else. Those moments are private, like the letters to us that have remained secret.

Today, I am shuffling around the house, listening to a Sufi song on YouTube. One Sara used to listen to. It's not for me as much as it's for the baby. I rub my six-month swelled belly. I coo to the harmony of the song. Child, it took three parents to make you. Anything is possible in this world you will grow in. It's important for any child to know its roots. One day, this child will know how it came into this world.

There is only one fear that occasionally swirls in my heart. And that is the blood of my mother. How it may change me once our baby is born. But these fears are fleeting. Because in the end, there is Sara. Sara was always there, before Ketan, after Ketan, and after she left. Sara's always becoming. And that's what we'll tell our child.

Acknowledgments

It takes a village to raise a book. We're told writers create in isolation, but that's only technically true. The creation itself comes from our engagement with the world, the relationships we create, build, destroy, and even imagine. It takes a village to consider a book and to inspire the writer in unlikely moments. It takes the potency of our collective imagination to allow for one perspective to manifest as a book. This is why it's impossible to thank every person responsible for this book to be published. Some people and environments are tucked deep into my subconscious mind.

And yet, there are so many lovely, amazing people who had a direct influence on this book.

My mother, Rosemary Mukherjee, for the love, the wings, and the constant generosity. Indrayudh Ghoshal, my partner who builds life with me and offers me a new way to evolve every day.

Kirsten Lepionka, my Pitch Wars mentor, who truly nourished this book with love and fierce insight. My agent, Stacy Testa, who made me believe in people who choose a profession via heart, soul, and passion. I thank you for the countless insights and utter belief that this "strange little book" would find its home.

Chris Heiser, for the tremendous editing process that allowed me to expand slumping narratives and straighten up sagging sentences. The editorial eye is truly the one that allows for readers to be present in every paragraph they read. Olivia Smith for the roaring enthusiasm and marketing support. Jaya Nicely for the stunning cover art.

Kalabati Majumdar, for the creative life we've built together and for the oodles of love.

Julie Carrick Dalton, for the unlikely email friendship and the amount of support you've given me during the birthing of this book.

The faculty and friends from my time in CCA in San Francisco, for the foundation that let me imagine what life could be as a writer, and for all the vision and countless classes that allowed me to dream big enough.

Nisha Abdullah, for reading the first draft of this book. Michelle D'Costa, for being my first public reader and cheerleader.

Paromita Dhar, because of her unabashed opinion on what I had to do with my life. Arun Nagarajan, for the early years of complete and utter belief. Disha and Kaushik Chatterjee, for the tight security of family. Pallavi Chander, for the woo-woo conversations that help me conquer the walls of pure rationality with more imagination. Manjiri Indurkar, for manifesting as a true writing friend.

The Pitch Wars community and my past students at Bangalore Writers Workshop for the support, love, and community.

A special thanks to Tom Roach for an essay excerpt I used that was published in *Friendship as a Way of Life: Foucault, AIDS, and the Politics of Shared Estrangement*, published by State University of New York Press in 2012, and to translator Daniel Ladinsky for his translated poems by Hafiz.

I thank the internet and all the creative giving that is channeled on it for allowing me to become an expert in philosophy for a brief period of time.

I've missed many others who have participated in my life as a writer and, as a result, this book. I hope they will know who they are and will feel my gratitude.

About the Author

Rheea Mukherjee received her MFA from California College of the Arts in San Francisco. Her fiction and nonfiction has been published in Scroll.in, *Southern Humanities Review*, *Out of Print*, *QLRS* and *Bengal Lights*, among others. Her previous stories have been Pushcart nominees, Glimmer Train Very Short Fiction Finalists, and semi-finalists for the Black Lawrence Press Award. Rheea spent her childhood in the US and her teens in India. She currently resides in Bangalore where she co-founded Bangalore Writers Workshop in 2012, and co-runs Write Leela Write, a Design and Content Laboratory. *The Body Myth* is her first novel. You can learn more at www.rheeamukherjee.com.